"So what's on the agenda for tonight, my lowly ladies-in-waiting?" asked Nesta.

"Becca's dad is bringing Mac and Squidge up with Bec," replied Lia. "So I guess the usual. Eat, drink, and be merry."

"Mac was telling us about that game you guys play down here," said Lucy. "Truth, Dare, Kiss, or Promise. Can we play that?"

Lia and I groaned. "Oh, noooooo," I said. "We've all had enough of that game. Let's do something else."

"Oh, pleeeeeese?" begged Lucy. "Just one go each. Just to see what it's like. Oh, come on, it will be a laugh. . . ."

"Maybe they don't want to reveal any deep, dark secrets in the truth option," said Izzie.

"No," I said. "It's not that. We are all mates together."

All Mates Together

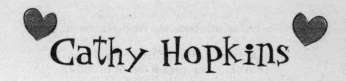

Cathy Hopkins

Simon Pulse
New York   London   Toronto   Sydney

SIMON PULSE
An imprint of Simon & Schuster
Children's Publishing Division
1230 Avenue of the Americas, New York, NY 10020

Copyright © 2006 by Cathy Hopkins
All rights reserved, including the right of reproduction in
whole or in part in any form.

SIMON PULSE and colophon are registered trademarks of
Simon and Schuster, Inc.

Designed by Karin Paprocki
The text of this book was set in Garamond 3.

Manufactured in the United States of America
First Simon Pulse edition April 2007
2 4 6 8 10 9 7 5 3 1

Library of Congress Control Number 2006940342
ISBN-13: 978-1-4169-2722-8
ISBN-10: 1-4169-2722-0

Big thanks to Brenda Gardner, Anne Clark, and all the fab team at Piccadilly. And thanks as always to Steve Loverling for all his support and help, especially in accompanying me to all the locations in the book and taking photos of them.

All Mates
Together

At Last!

"I NEVER THOUGHT THIS would really happen," I said as I looked around at what was left of my bedroom. It was so neat and tidy. Usually it was jampacked with stuff: clothes and shoes spilling out of the wardrobe, posters of the latest pin-ups fighting for space on the wall, books and magazines weighing down the tiny shelf above the radiator, and Emma's dolls, pencils, and crayons cluttering up the floor. Most of it had now been packed away and all that was left were the bunk beds, empty drawers, and shelves.

"We'll come and help you move into the new place, too," said Becca, who had come over with Lia early that morning to give a hand with last-minute jobs.

"When is D for departure day?" asked Lia.

"Day after tomorrow," I said. "And I can't wait!

At last, at last, at laaaaaaaaaaaaaaast, a room of my own. Not that I don't love Emma, I do. 'Course I do. But hey, share a room with my kid sister and have jellybeans stuck to my bed covers for the rest of my life? I don't think so. It's going to be so brilliant decorating how I want and well . . . just having some space to myself for a change."

Becca and Lia are my best friends. Becca has been since junior school and Lia since the beginning of Year Nine, almost a year ago when she came down from London to live here in Cornwall. Both of them have had their own rooms forever, so I don't think that they really know what it's like to share a room with a six-year-old psychopath. I've had to share with her since I was nine, just before Mum died and everything changed forever.

"So have you thought about a color scheme for your new room yet?" asked Becca as she pulled her long hair back up into a clip. She has fab hair. It's the most amazing color: like a red setter dog's, rich and glossy—unlike mine, which is short and dark and boooooring unless I spike it up.

"I keep changing my mind," I said. "I want you

guys to see the room before I decide anything. Plus Jen said that sometimes it's a good idea to live in a place for a few weeks before making up your mind. Get the feel of it, you know?"

Jen is Dad's fiancée, soon-to-be wife. She is coming to live with us at the new house, and she and Dad are going to get married at the end of the summer holidays, which is in about four weeks' time.

"My mum says that about pets," said Lia. "When we got our pot-bellied pig, she said to live with him for a while and the right name would come. Then we found out that he was a she, so it was a good job that we didn't name her too soon."

I laughed. Their pet pig is called Lola. Lia's dad named her. He said she reminded him of one of his fans who used to run around after him wearing pink high-heels. Lia's dad is Zac Axford, the famous rock star. The Axford family are the most glamorous family in the whole of Cornwall. They live in a massive house, the size of a hotel, and have a garden the size of a small country. Lia's totally normal though—personality-wise anyway, but in the looks department she's stunning. Tall, slim, white-blond hair, silver-blue eyes. Most boys' fantasy girl, as far as I can make out. I've seen them when she walks past. It's hysterical. They look at her like their eyes are about to pop out of their sockets and their tongues fall out onto the floor. Not that she notices. Lia says she thinks she looks like a duck and has no boobs. Funny how no one is happy with the way they look. Like Becca: She's really pretty, too, but she thinks she's fat when actually she's curvy. Mad. They both look fab.

Becca looked thoughtful for a moment as she looked round my room. "It will be strange you living somewhere new. It's like I've always known you here. Always come here after school."

"I know, but hey, you can come for sleepovers at my new house now without having to share a sleeping bag with one of Emma's Barbie dolls and a My Little Pony stuck in your ear. It has five bedrooms: one for Dad and Jen, one for Luke, one for Joe, one for Emma, and one for me. The boys are really looking forward to having their own rooms, too—they're going to be on the top floor. Dad even said that maybe we can get a kitten when we're settled in. It's going to be brill for all of us."

I was glad that Dad was marrying Jen. I liked her and she'd never tried to act as if she was our new mum. She made it clear from the beginning that she understood that Mum could never be replaced. Jen works as an air hostess and, up until recently, she flew all over the world. After we move, though, she's only going to do internal flights that go from Newquay to other parts of England so that she's never away for too long. Dad wanted her to give up altogether and help him run the village shop, but she said no, that being together twenty-four hours a day is a recipe for relationship disaster, whereas absence makes the heart grow fonder. I think she is very wise and am glad she'll be coming to live with us. As well as being a good cook, she makes Dad laugh, and it's great to see him happy and smartening himself up a bit. His hair got all straggly round the collar at one point, but now he has it cut regularly, and in his new jeans and shirts he looks halfway decent for a grown-up. For a long time after Mum died he was so sad and quiet and didn't seem to bother about how he looked. Like all the life had gone out of him. He tried to act as if he was okay, but I could tell that he wasn't. It hit him hard. He threw himself into his work and kept himself busy all the time, but I think he was mainly doing it so that he wouldn't have to think too much about the fact that Mum had gone.

I had to help out a lot in the house, because he was working at the shop so much. That's another reason I am glad that Jen is moving in—she can help with some of the household chores. Luke is eleven and Joe is nine and Emma's six, almost seven. That means a ton of laundry, a ton of washing up, and mountains of food to be bought and prepared. I don't know what's happened to Luke and Joe lately, but all they seem to do is eat and eat and eat. Toast and peanut butter and crisps and chips and sausages and pasta, but they never seem to get much fatter. As the eldest in our family, and seeing as we had no mum, I have had to do a *lot* of babysitting and housework. It is going to be sooooooooo brill to be able to be a normal teenager at last.

At that moment, Dad popped his head round the door.

"Hey, girls," he said. "Seeing as most of the kitchen is packed up and you girls are all going to be at your sleepover supper later at Lia's, I'm going out to get some pizza. I'm taking the boys and Em with me so that you can get on without them under your feet, Cat. Okay?"

"Okay, Dad. What's still to be done?"

Dad shrugged. "Not sure. Maybe you could go from room to room and make a list, then we'll divide up what's left of the tasks later."

After they'd gone, I got a piece of paper and began to make a list.

Bathroom: Pack up last bits of toiletries. Clean. Make sure wet towels are put in separate bag from dry towels.

Hallway: don't forget coats and jackets, welly boots.

"Most of it seems to be sorted," said Lia as we went from room to room.

Becca nodded and laughed as she came out of Luke and Joe's room. "Wow! I don't think I have ever seen that room look like anything but a bomb-site. Amazing!"

"Hey, don't forget the lamp shades," said Lia, pointing up to the ceiling. "You don't want to leave those."

I looked up to where she'd pointed. "Oh, yeah. Thanks, we'd have completely forgotten those and—OH!"

"What?" asked Lia. "What?"

I pointed back up at the ceiling. "Up there. We'd all forgotten. The stupid loft! There's a whole *pile* of stuff up there. Oh, *no*. Just when I thought we were almost done."

Becca's face lit up. "Hey! Maybe we'll find forgotten treasure up there," she said. "You read about it all the time in books . . ."

"Or fabulous old paintings that are worth a fortune," said Lia, "or an antique that is worth millions and is taken on to one of those TV shows where it's valued . . ."

I laughed. "Not in our loft, I don't think! It's where all the rubbish has been shoved over the years, so don't get too carried away. I can tell you that all we're going to find up there are bags of old clothes that should have been thrown out for the jumble, some old camping equipment, and basically stuff no one wanted but couldn't be bothered to throw out. Still, better bring it down. I doubt if the new owner is going to want to find their new loft full of trash."

"Where's the ladder?" asked Becca. "I'm not giving up hope. You might not have looked properly."

"Yeah right," I said as I fetched the ladder from behind the door in Dad's room and placed it in the hall under the loft hole.

"I think there's a light switch up there on the left-hand side," I said as Becca climbed up first and clambered in.

Lia went next and I was last.

Becca turned the switch on and the space was illuminated, showing the inside of the roof, bits of old wiring, wooden joists running across the floor then in the corners under the eaves, piles of cardboard boxes and bags.

We looked in the first group of boxes and, sure enough, they were full of old junk: goggles, snorkeling gear, flippers, an old Monopoly set, books, magazines, old shoes . . . Even Becca began to lose interest after a while when she realized that there wasn't much of interest in there and certainly no evidence of valuable antiques or paintings, although there was a sketch pad of some of my early drawings from junior school.

"They'll be worth a fortune one day," I said as I tucked the pad under my arm and headed back down the ladder.

We worked for the next hour passing the boxes and bags along and down into the hall. I stood at the bottom of the ladder and Lia and Becca passed stuff down to me from above.

"Last one," called Lia finally. "It's only a plastic bag. Think there are sleeping bags in there. Watch out, I'm going to drop it."

She let the bag go and it fell with a soft thud on to the carpet next to me.

"Okay, coming down," said Lia. "Come on, Bec. Hey, hold on a mo, Cat, Becca's disappeared. Bec? What is it?"

Lia disappeared from the loft hole. I could hear rustlings and their voices up above, but I couldn't hear what they were saying.

"Hey, Lia, Becca, you okay up there?" I asked as I began to climb the ladder.

Suddenly Becca's face appeared at the hole. She looked flushed with excitement. "Hey, Cat, get up here. I think we've found something!"

2 All Mates Together

A CAR TOOTED OUTSIDE the house. Lia went and looked out of the window. "Our lift's here," she said. "Hurry up."

"But I can't find my pajamas," I said as I rooted around in one of the big plastic bags that I'd stuffed some of my clothes in ready for the move. "I can't find *anything*, in fact."

"Don't worry, I can lend you whatever you need," said Lia, "but we need to get going, as I said we'd pick the London girls up on the way."

Becca had left over half an hour ago to go back to her house to collect her things for the sleepover, and was meeting us up at Lia's. I grabbed my toothbrush from the bathroom and five minutes later we were speeding away, rock-star style, in a sleek black BMW to pick up our new pals: TJ, Nesta, Izzie, and Lucy. Traveling in one of the Axfords' cars never ceased to be a thrill as it was such a change from my normal ride, bouncing around in the back of Dad's shop van with boxes full of tins of tomatoes, cat food, or bottled water for company. Dad's van stank of gasoline and old boots; the BMW smelled of leather, aftershave, and money.

I put on my sunglasses and grinned at Lia. "This is the life," I said. "I think I was born to live this kind of way."

Lia grinned back. She really *was* born to live that way.

Lucy, TJ, Nesta, and Izzie were waiting for us in the early-evening sunshine in the driveway outside the holiday cottage that TJ's parents had recently bought and where the girls were staying. The Axfords' chauffeur (who was a local nineteen-year-old boy called Stuart) looked like he'd died and gone to heaven when an avalanche of pretty, perfumed, lip-glossed girls burst into the car. Izzie dived in the front (she's the tallest) and Lucy, Nesta, and TJ squeezed in with Lia and me in the back.

"Seatbelts, girls," said Stuart, and there was

another commotion as everyone squirmed about finding them, then clicking them on.

"Super-spiffing and fabola," said Nesta in a false posh voice as we set off once again. "Right ho, chaps, let's go for tiffin at the Axfords'."

"Yah. Top-ho and super-marvelous bumper bazzing," said Lucy in an equally daft voice. "Oh my loid, did anyone put my daaaaahling corgis in the back?"

"I do hope so, my dear," said Izzie, also in a very snooty voice. "Or else it's dead-dog meat for tea."

"Oh not again," said Nesta. "Dog meat is so frightfully common, especially when served with white bread, and it just doesn't go with cucumber."

TJ rolled her eyes. "Pardon my mad friends, they're having a competition to see who can speak most like the Queen," she explained.

"Okaaaaay," laughed Lia as Nesta did a royal wave out of the window at passersby.

I only met these girls recently, but already we're all good mates. TJ was first down last Easter and we bumped into each other on the beach one afternoon. Her dad was ill at the time and she was having a cry about it. What was so totally amazing was that she was in *my* secret crying place. It's an area on Cawsand Bay that's hidden away from the rest of the beach, and it's where I go when I'm feeling freaked out or missing Mum. We got on immediately, and what was even more incredible was that we discovered that we had both been seeing Lia's elder brother, Ollie. Neither of us knew about the other, and it all backfired on him, because TJ and I became friends and we both blew Ollie out. TJ's dad got better and her parents fell in love with the area, bought a cottage as a second home, and the rest of the girls came down for the summer hols.

They're a fab bunch and we get on brilliantly, even though they are a year older than Lia, Bec, and I. They exude city sophistication. Nesta is totally awesome to look at. She's gorgeous, with long black hair and a perfect body. I think her mum's Jamaican and her dad's Italian, which is why she looks so exotic. If she wasn't so nice and funny, I would have to kill her. Izzie is the tallest of the four and is one of the most interesting girls I have ever met. She's into so many things I never even heard of until I met her: New Age stuff, crystals and witch-craft and astrology. She's also got a pierced belly-but-ton, which looks way cool. TJ and Izzie have both got dark hair, but Izzie's is more chestnut-colored and she has the most amazing green eyes. Lucy is small with blond hair and has a great laugh. She's the fashion expert out of all of them and wants to be a designer when she leaves school. She's sooo stylish and I hope one day that she'll give me some advice, because we're about the same height and she really knows how to dress. TJ is probably the most sensible of the four of them, but only just. She can be pretty mad too, although mainly she's just a sweetie.

"So what's on the agenda for tonight, my lowly ladies-in-waiting?" asked Nesta.

"Becca's dad is bringing Mac and Squidge up with Bec," replied Lia, "so I guess the usual: eat, drink, and be merry."

"Mac was telling us about that game you guys play down here," said Lucy. "Truth, Dare, Kiss, or Promise. Can we play that?"

Lia and I groaned. "Oh noooooo," I said. "We've

all had enough of that game. Let's do something else."

"Oh pleeeeeese," begged Lucy. "Just one go each. Just to see what it's like. Oh, come on, it will be a laugh . . ."

"Maybe they don't want to reveal any deep dark secrets in the Truth option," said Izzie.

"No," I said, "it's not that. We are all mates together."

"So let's do it then," said Izzie. "We'll be back to school in London soon and won't see you for ages . . ."

"As Queen, I decree it," Nesta announced in her royal voice. "I hereby demand by law that all my royal subjects shall play Truth, Dare, Kiss, or Promise, and anyone who tries to bunk out shall be executed and their heads chopped off and displayed on the lawn with a daffodil stuck in their gobette. So there. Amen. And forthwith, etc."

Lia and I laughed. "Yes, Your Majesty," we chorused. "We don't want to be dead now, do we?"

"Not at such a young age," said Lia.

In the mirror, I could see that Stuart was having

a hard time not bursting out laughing. He must have thought we were all totally bonkers.

As soon as Mac and Squidge arrived at Lia's, they were made to kneel at Nesta's feet and be knighted. Seeing as Queen Nesta didn't have a proper sword, she used a soup ladle as it was the nearest thing handy. Neither of them objected for a second, as even though they are both sixteen and older than the rest of us, they are in awe of Nesta's gorgeousness. Seeing them act so tongue-tied reminded me of when Lia first arrived at our school last September. They went ga-ga stupid then too. She and Squidge have been an item for ages now and it's clearly true love on both sides, but sometimes I catch him looking at her like he can't quite believe his luck. I can. Squidge is one of the nicest boys on the planet. I know because I've known him most of my life and we were even an item for a while. Everyone loves him. And Lia is one of the nicest girls. She's so gentle and considerate. They are a match made in heaven. Mac is Squidge's best mate. He's cute-looking too, only smaller than

Squidge, and he's blond whereas Squidge has dark hair, at least most of the time he does. His mum is the local hairdresser and likes to experiment from time to time and, of course, she always nabs Squidge to try styles and colors out on. He doesn't mind. He's so easy-going, she could shave his hair off and he'd just shrug and say, "Yeah, cool." And he'd probably make it cool too. He's that kind of boy.

After the knighting ceremony, we had a fab supper of burgers, chunky chips, and pecan fudge ice cream served up by Meena the housekeeper. The kitchen is vast, bigger than the whole of the ground floor of the house we're about to leave. And it's wonderfully light, from skylights in the ceiling and floor-to-ceiling glass doors that lead out on to an enormous patio that is the length of the whole house.

After second helpings of ice cream, we had to go and lie down to recover in the red room, so called because it is mainly red: red walls, wine-red curtains—the walls are honey-colored though. With the oak flooring and Turkish rugs, the whole effect is rich and warm and exotic.

"Our sitting room at home is done in these colors," said Nesta as she reclined Cleopatra-style on one of the sofas.

"I've been trying to persuade Dad and Jen to have a red room in our new house," I said, "but I don't think Dad's that fussed about décor. He says that with four children, nowhere is going to stay looking that smart for long."

"Well at least you can make your room how you like," said Lucy. "That's what I try to do. People can do what they like in the rest of the house—and believe me, my two brothers do—but my room is my private territory. I have a warning sign on the door saying: KEEP OUT on pain of death."

"Great idea. I'll have one made," I said.

"Okay, so what sort of thing do you dare each other in the Truth, Dare game?" asked TJ as the rest of us settled on various sofas and cushions around the room.

"Oh, to jump off cliffs, parachute out of planes," said Squidge, "that's the sort of thing we usually do."

Izzie's jaw dropped open. "Really?"

"No. No way," said Becca. "We do normal stuff—like, these guys dared me to go into the Pop Princess competition just before Christmas last year. If it wasn't for them, I wouldn't have had the nerve."

Becca has a great voice and we had all gone up for the competition with her. She was the only one that made it through, though, and she got as far as third place.

"Oh and there was all that trouble with Lia's turn," said Mac. "She got the Kiss option and had to kiss Jonno Appleton, the school heart-throb . . ."

"Yeah, but the school bully wasn't too happy," said Becca, "because she fancied Jonno herself and she made Lia's life miserable for a while."

Lia grimaced and Squidge put a protective arm round her. "I don't want to hear about creeps like him or her."

"And then there was the time I was dared to tell the truth about something," I said, "and I got into a real tizz about truth and lies. Like—I always thought I was a truthful person, but in one week I counted about fifteen lies and realized that I was the Fibbing Fibster from Fibville."

"Lies like what?" asked Izzie.

"Oh you know, lying about my age to get into the movies . . ."

"We *all* do that," everyone chorused.

"What else?" asked Nesta.

"Not wanting to hurt anyone's feelings, not wanting to own up that I hadn't done my homework or to Dad that I'd been watching X-rated horror DVDs. Not major lies, but all the same, made me think. I decided to tell the absolute truth the following week and almost lost all my friends because I was so blunt—like if your best mate has a pimple on her nose and asks if it looks really bad, what do you say? 'No,' which makes you a liar, or yes, and she won't speak to you anymore."

"I guess there has to be a halfway measure," said Lucy.

"Maybe. That's pretty well what I decided. Maybe white lies," I said.

"So what else?" asked Nesta. "Sounds like

you've been getting up to all sorts down here."

Mac laughed. "Yeah. Someone should write a series of books about it. I was dared to go for a cartooning job, and that was cool, because like Becca, I might not have had the nerve otherwise."

"Did you get it?" asked Izzie. "The job?"

Mac looked so chuffed that she'd asked him. "Yeah, actually I did," he said.

"Becca told me that you're a brilliant cartoonist," said Izzie. "I'd love to see some of your work before we go back to London."

Mac looked even more chuffed. "Yeah. Right. Whenever. I mean . . . sure, I'd be glad to show you."

Becca shot me a knowing look. We had only been talking that afternoon about the fact that we had noticed that there was some major chemistry happening between Izzie and Mac. Becca thought Mac needed some encouragement though, as he had had a few knock-backs in the love game of late and his confidence had been a bit dented.

"Sounds good, this game," said Izzie. "Sounds like it's made you all feel the fear and do it anyway."

According to Lucy, *Feel the Fear and Do It Anyway* was one of Izzie's favorite books. She has promised to lend me it sometime, which is brill, as it sounds like Izzie knows a lot about good books to help people get on with what they want in their lives.

"Yeah. Sounds like fun," said Nesta. "What about you, Squidge?"

"Lia and I have mainly gone for the Promise option and promised to tell the truth and be faithful. Stuff like that," said Squidge.

"Ahhh," sighed all the girls.

Mac rolled his eyes. "Pass me the sick bucket," he said.

"Hey, Bec, you going to tell them the truth about the last time we played?" I asked.

Becca blushed, looked at the floor then up at Lucy. "It was when you and your family first arrived down here at the beginning of the hols," she said. "Remember I grabbed your brother Lal as soon as he set foot on the beach and kissed him?"

"Yeah. He was well made up. Why? Was that a dare?"

Becca nodded. "See, I'd been going on about how I was through with boys forever, and the others said no way, and Squidge said I had to kiss the next boy who came on to the beach."

Lucy began laughing. "I did wonder what was going on. And so did Mum and Dad. I remember Dad saying that he thought the Cornish girls were very forward. Shame it wasn't Steve, hey?"

"Well, I got to the right brother in the end," said Becca.

After the kiss, Becca dated Lal for a couple of weeks, but then cooled off him. Then she met Lucy's other brother, Steve, and really liked him, but didn't think anything would come of it because she didn't want to hurt anyone's feelings. Luckily, Lal fell for a local girl called Shazza, and Steve and Becca got together for the few days that he was still down here before he went back up to London. They're going to stay in touch, though, and no doubt both Steve and Lal will be back down again now as their parents really love the place and have already talked about future holidays down here.

"Okay, so that just about brings you up to date on our Truth, Dare experiences," I said. "Now, which one of you wants to go first?"

"Me," blurted Mac before anyone could say anything. "And I dare Squidge . . ."

"Oh *no*," groaned Squidge. "Look mate, we're playing this for Izzie, Nesta, Lucy, and TJ. Let them have a go."

"I will," said Mac, "but first you've got to agree to get back on your bike."

For a moment, there was an awkward silence. Squidge had a bad accident in May and came off his bike. He was in a plaster cast for ages and only had it taken off just over a week ago. All of us had noticed that he hadn't been back on his bike, but no one dared say anything until now.

"You don't have to," said Lia. "You don't ever have to get back on that bike again."

Squidge took a deep breath. "I do. No, I do. Get back on the horse, back on the bike, etc., etc. Yeah. I will."

"When?" insisted Mac.

Lucy laughed. "Wow. You're as bossy as Nesta, and we thought *she* was bad."

"Hey," Nesta objected, "I'm not bossy. I just know what's best for people."

"Exactly," said Mac. "So when, Squidge?"

"Tomorrow. I'll do it."

I felt for Squidge. Usually he's Mr. Fearless, Mr. Try Anything, but the accident had left him shaken.

"I've got some stuff that might help you," said Izzie. "It's called Rescue Remedy and if you take it when you need a shot of confidence, it really helps."

"What is it?" asked Becca. "Is it like medicine?"

"Not really. It's made from flower essences discovered by someone called Dr. Bach, so it's all completely natural. There are loads of remedies for all sorts of things—like anxiety, sadness, lack of confidence, and so on. The list is endless."

Once again, I felt in awe of Izzie. Like Becca, I had never heard of Dr. Bach, but I was well impressed.

"Okay, enough hocus-pocus," said Nesta. "Who's next?"

"Me," said Izzie.

"Okay," said Becca. "Truth, Dare, Kiss, or Promise?"

"Kiss," said Izzie and gave Mac a very flirtatious look.

"Okay," said Becca. "You have to kiss Mac. Right now."

Izzie gave Mac a look that was a cross between a dare and a come-on, while Mac blushed beet red. However he did get up, cross the room, take Izzie's hand, and pull her to her feet. She stood up so that they were facing, well, almost—he was actually an inch or two smaller than her. I noticed her bend her knees slightly so that she was the same height as he was and then they kissed . . . and kissed . . . and kissed . . .

"Pheeeeew! Getting *hot* in here," laughed Squidge as we watched Mac and Izzie go for an Oscar-winning clench.

"Ten . . . nine . . . eight . . . seven . . . six . . . five . . . four . . . three . . .two . . . one . . ." Lucy counted down and we all clapped in time to the numbers.

"Oh get a *rooooooom*," chorused TJ and Nesta.

Mac and Izzie broke apart and looked around at us. Both of them looked dazed, as if they had been hit by lightning or something. As the game continued, Mac stayed sitting next to Izzie and held her hand the whole time.

After that, Nesta got the Promise option, so we made her promise to keep coming down to Cornwall after she's famous—which I have no doubt she will be one day. She has the air of a celebrity about her already.

Lucy was dared to stand on her head and sing "God Save the Queen," which she did with great style. Apparently it's one of her party pieces up in London.

TJ got the Truth option.

"What is the most important thing in your life?" asked Nesta. "And you have to tell us the truth, the whole truth, and nothing but the truth."

"Easy," said TJ. "My mates. Yeah, my family and my dog, Mojo, too—but mainly my mates."

"Ahhhh," chorused all the girls.

"You girls are so wet," said Mac, only to be greeted by a barrage of cushions and pillows that then escalated into a brilliant pillow fight. Lucy was a force to be reckoned with. For someone so small, she could pack a punch. "Comes from having brothers," she said as she blasted Mac around the head.

It was only much later, when the girls were settling down into sleeping bags, that Becca remembered what we had found in the loft. It always makes me laugh when we have a sleepover at the Axfords' because each of us could have our own room with its own telly and bathroom, but we still choose to sleep in one room on the floor in sleeping bags so that we can all be together. Apart from Squidge and Mac, that is; they get relegated to a boys' room as Mr Axford says he doesn't want any "hanky-panky" going on.

"Hey, Cat, did you get that box open after I'd gone?" asked Becca as she snuggled in on the floor next to me.

"Nope," I said. "Not yet. I couldn't find the key, but it has to turn up somewhere."

"What box?" asked Nesta.

"We were clearing out the loft earlier and found—well, it's not really a box," I explained, "it's made out of metal, like an old toolbox, only bigger. It's like a metal trunk."

"It was behind the water tank," said Lia, "and looked like it hadn't been touched for years."

"Oh wow, how fantastic," said Izzie. "A mystery."

"Yeah. Fabola," said Nesta.

"Any idea what might be in it?" asked TJ.

"Not really," I said, although secretly I did. Becca and Lia hadn't noticed, but I had straight away. Two letters were painted in red on the side of the trunk: *L.M.* I was sure it was L.M. for Laura Morgan. Morgan was my mum's maiden name. Laura was her first name. The box had belonged to my mother. I had no idea what might be in there, but I knew that if and when I got it open, I wanted to be on my own.

"Hey, Cat. Truth, Dare, Kiss, Promise?" said Izzie.

"Er . . . promise."

"Okay. You have to promise to tell us what's in the box as soon as you find out. I can't bear an unsolved mystery."

"Sure," I promised. But no one could see that I had my fingers crossed. There might be anything in that box for all I knew.

Garage Sale

"Is that the last load?" asked Luke as I passed him a black bin bag from the back of the van.

"Yep," I said and jumped out the back, ready to help Dad set the stall up. "Let the sale commence."

"Yeah, let's get it over with so I can get back to my PlayStation," said Joe. "I think it's rotten the way Dad treats us like his personal slaves."

"Oi, I heard that," said Dad, appearing from the front of the van. "And why shouldn't I treat you as my personal slaves when that's exactly what you are? No point in having kids if they're not going to do chores for you. Now, snap to it everyone and let's make some dosh." He rubbed his hands together, tousled Joe's hair, and began to set out our make-do sales table, which was actually a wallpapering table with a sheet over it.

It was Saturday afternoon and luckily the good

weather continued to hold, as our family had joined the crowds of others gathered at Maker Heights for one of the biggest garage sales in the area. We had a ton of junk to sell: old toys, books, magazines, a pile of the stuff from the loft, utensils, crockery, tools from the garage—you name it . . . Jen had been over earlier in the week and gone through everything that was to be taken to the new house with a fine-toothed comb. She had been horrified at the state of most of the kitchen stuff and insisted that more than half of it was chucked—partly because she had her own set of kitchen things, which was more modern and stylish, and partly because she said that she wanted to get some things for the new place, that were hers and Dad's together, not his or hers from their past lives. "It's to be a fresh start," she said. "A new chapter in all of our lives." Dad, who has a hard time throwing anything away, had intervened on the chucking-out idea and suggested that we do a garage sale instead.

Like all events in the Rame Peninsula, most of the village was there—including all my mates and the London girls, who seemed well impressed at the scale of it. There must have been over two hundred cars and vans parked with stalls set out in front of them.

Izzie, Lucy, TJ, and Nesta had got there early and had already been round the sale. They'd bought a variety of CDs, DVDs, and junk. Lucy was over the moon with some vintage clothing she had found on one stall.

"I know the dresses aren't exactly the latest thing," she said as she showed us her spoils, "but the fabrics and the buttons are priceless. You couldn't buy them these days. I think these are from the 1950s. Fab. They cost a fortune up in London, because everyone is after stuff like this."

"We've finished here so we're heading over to the beach at Whitsand," said Izzie. "Want to join us later?"

"Maybe," I said. "Depends on how this goes. I have to man the stall as Dad can only stay an hour, because the girl who was minding his shop is only there until twelve."

"What about your brothers and Emma? Aren't

they here to help?" asked TJ as she pointed to Luke, Joe, and Emma, who had decided to put on some of the old clothes that we were going to sell. Emma had a colander on her head and was wearing an old toweling dressing-gown that trailed on the ground and was way too long for her six-year-old body. Joe had a pan on his head and was pretending to be a Dalek from *Doctor Who*, and Luke had one of our old Halloween vampire masks on and was frightening off anyone who tried to come near the stall.

"Er . . . maybe not . . ." said Lucy. 'They look about as helpful as my brothers are at this sort of thing."

"Exactly," I said. "Don't worry, Mac and Squidge will be here later too."

At the mention of Mac, Izzie perked up. "Mac and Squidge?"

I nodded. "Lia and Becca have gone over to Plymouth, but the boys promised they'd come."

"Er . . . maybe we could drop back later and give you a hand clearing up, eh?" said Izzie.

"Sure," I said.

"Call my mobile," said Izzie.

"Yeah, because she really really wants to help you clear up," said Nesta. "It's not because Mac is going to be here or anything . . ."

Lucy gave her a light slap on her arm. "Give her a break, Nesta. It's love. Don't interfere."

"I wasn't," Nesta objected. "I was merely stating the obvious."

"Which is obvious," said Lucy as she motioned zipping her lips. "So shut it."

"Later," said TJ as the girls headed off down the hill, still squabbling as they went.

Halfway down the hill, Izzie turned and held up her mobile. "Call me," she mouthed.

The first couple of hours of the sale went by in a flash and we sold almost three-quarters of the stuff, but not without having to make some severe reductions. It was amazing. Some items we were virtually giving away, but people still wanted to bargain and knock the price down.

We sold jigsaw puzzles, a lamp without a shade, a tatty old bath mat, a teapot that was missing its lid. Seemed that everything was wanted by someone.

Joe and Emma were hopeless, but Luke turned out to be a great salesperson and he was tough with the old dears who were trying to get what they could for free.

"Whoa! *Joe, NO!*" I called out as I spotted that he was about to put out a bag of clothes that wasn't to be sold. I had put the bag aside in the upstairs hall before we left in the morning and had meant to put it in the sitting room with the other bags ready to take to the new house. I hadn't noticed that somehow it had been brought up to the car boot sale instead.

"What?" he asked as he threw his arms up in the air. "What am I doing wrong now?"

"Nothing," I said as I rescued the bag from him. "Just that lot's not for sale."

"Oh pardon me for trying to be helpful," he said.

I took the bag from him and put it back into the van, then stuck a Post-it note on it saying: *Not For Sale!!!*

It wasn't as if there was anything valuable in there, but the clothes were precious to me. They had belonged to Mum and I had kept them tucked away in my wardrobe for years. Dad had put them aside after her death and had meant to either give them to someone we knew or take them to a charity shop. I had stolen them and hidden them. I'm sure that Dad knew they were there, but he never said anything. They were all that I had left of her, apart from a few photos in the albums and the shoebox in which I kept a few trinkets: bits of her old jewelry, an empty bottle of the perfume she used to wear (Mitsouko by Guerlain), and a letter she'd written when she knew that she was ill and might not recover. She'd asked Dad to give it to me just before I started secondary school. The letter was one of my greatest treasures. I'd read it so many times, I knew it off by heart.

> *My darling girl,*
> *All grown up and ready to start a new school,*
> *and how I wish I was going to be there to see it. I*
> *wanted to write to you and tell you how proud I*
> *am of you. You have been a strength to me over*
> *the last year and the light of my days. Be strong,*
> *Cat. Be true to yourself and always be brave, as*
> *I know you will be. God bless. My love will*
> *always be with you,*
> *Your mum*

My mum. I knew so little about her. Who she was. What had made her laugh and cry. I couldn't remember. Sometimes I wondered what she was like at my age—did she have crushes or feel awkward or shy about anything? What was she into? I was sad that I could never ask her.

"So, who's hungry?" asked Dad, coming back laden with food from a stall on the next aisle over. He began handing it out. "A doughnut for Emma. Bacon sandwiches for the rest of us."

Joe and Luke took theirs and began tucking in energetically. I put mine aside.

"Not eating, Cat?" Dad asked.

I shook my head. Actually I had decided that I might be vegetarian. It was another of the things that impressed me about Izzie. She didn't make a song or dance about it or try to lay it on anyone and make them feel guilty about eating meat, but I'd noticed that she didn't, and when I asked her about it, she said that she couldn't bear to eat anything that had once had a pulse and breathed. I had never even thought about it before, but the more I did, the more I wanted to be vegetarian as well. However, as the alluring smell of bacon wafted up toward me, I decided that maybe I could make a new start in the new house. Part of the fresh chapter that Jen was on about. "Er—yes, thanks, Dad," I said and tucked in with the rest of them.

After a while, the first rush of eager buyers drifted off, the stalls grew quiet, and Dad went off to his shop for the afternoon.

"Go and have a quick look around, Cat," said Luke. "We can manage here."

"Thanks, kid," I said.

"I'm *not* a kid," said Luke. "You seem to forget that I am twelve now."

"Ooh, sorry."

Luke put his hands up to his ears and waggled them while sticking his tongue out.

"Yeah. Very grown up," I said and stuck my tongue out back at him.

Of course, Emma insisted on coming round the sale with me, and together we took off and cruised the stalls. It was an eye-opener to see what was on sale. You name it, it was there on someone's stall: kitchen stuff, bathroom stuff, tatty old curtains, linens, clothes, shoes, faded toys, DVDs, LPs, framed paintings, knickknacks, unwanted Christmas presents— even old buttons, screws, nuts, bolts, and bits of old cars! All aspects of people's lives laid out in front of them.

After looking around for half an hour, we headed back for our stall. From a distance, I could see that Mac and Squidge had arrived so I quickly called Izzie to let her know.

"I'm already on my way," she said. "It was too windy for me on the beach so I left the others. Be with you in a mo."

As I approached the stall, I could see, like Joe and Luke had done earlier, that Squidge and Mac thought it was a good idea to wear some of the clothes on sale. Squidge had on a pink blouse and skirt, and Mac was wearing a ladies' coat. I could see straight away whose clothes they were. Mum's. From the *Not For Sale!!!* bag. And Mac was about to sell one of her dresses to Mrs. McNelly from the post office.

"Nooooooooooooooooooooooo," I cried as I ran toward the stall and grabbed the dress. "No. You can't buy that."

Mrs. McNelly grabbed it back. "I saw it first. First come, first served."

I grabbed it back from her. "But you *can't*."

"Hey, Cat, the whole idea of one of these sales is that you sell the gear," said Squidge.

"But these things were my mum's. They weren't meant to be sold. In fact I put them in the van out of the way. Who got them out? Luke?"

"I didn't know," he said and for a moment, looked like he was going to cry. "I didn't know they were our mum's. You never said. I thought it was Jen's old stuff."

Mrs. McNelly immediately gave me back the dress. "Sorry, Cat, love, of course you have it," she said and scurried away. She had known my mum. Everyone in the village had.

"Have you sold anything else?" I asked.

Mac looked sheepish. "Jacket. Herringbone. Just now."

I thought I was going to burst into tears. "Please, *please*, get it back."

Mac set off down the hill at double-speed and almost knocked over Izzie, who was coming up toward us. He grabbed her hand. "Mission Recovery," he said and dragged her off.

Squidge and Luke were very sympathetic when they'd gone, and helped me fold up the rest of Mum's things that had been put out. Joe looked on with a strange expression on his face.

"Why didn't you tell us they were Mum's?" he asked.

"Er . . . I don't know. I guess I would have at some point," I replied.

Joe looked sad. "I can't remember her at all," he said after a short while. "Can't even picture her face."

I put my arm round him, but he shrugged me off and picked up one of Mum's shirts. He was only three when she died.

"I want to go home now," he said, and for a moment he looked so much younger than his nine years.

"Me too," said Emma. "This is booooring."

"Not much longer," I said. "But I guess we could start to pack up."

Mac and Izzie were back about twenty minutes later.

"Phew," said Mac. "Talk about a hard person to bargain with. The lady who bought the jacket wasn't local and she thought I was making it up about the jacket belonging to your dead mother . . . er—sorry, Cat, I mean—"

"I know," I said, and took the jacket from him. "It's okay. Thanks."

"Cost us five quid to get it back," said Izzie.

"And she only paid three quid for it." Mac sighed. "Talk about inflation."

"I'll give it to you out of our profits," I said. As I folded the jacket to put it back in with Mum's other things, I felt something in the pocket. I went round to the side of the van so that no one could see what I was doing and fished about to see what it was. I drew out a metal key. It looked exactly the right size to open Mum's trunk.

4 The Big Move

"CAT, WHERE'S THE COFFEE?" Jen called up the stairs.

"With the stuff in the box in the kitchen labeled *Shoe Cleaners*," I called back.

It was Sunday and the day of the move, everywhere was pandemonium and I'd been trying to get a moment to myself all morning. I closed the bedroom door and went back to Mum's trunk. I had hidden it under the bottom bunk with a couple of blankets over it so that no one would know that it was there. I meant to look at it the night before when I got back from saying goodbye to the London girls, who were preparing for their return home; however, with the last-minute packing and Dad insisting that Emma have an early night, there was no time alone in our room.

At last, a moment had presented itself in the

morning, when everyone was downstairs and I was by myself in the bedroom. I pulled the trunk out and knelt on the floor. I knew that I should tell Dad about it because there might be private stuff of Mum's in there. And I knew that at some time, I should tell Luke, Joe, and Emma. And I would. I just wanted a few moments alone with what I found first. I held my breath and tried the key in the lock. Bingo! It fitted. I was about to turn the key when there was another yell up the stairs.

"CAAAAAT! Where are the mugs? Have they *all* been packed?" Jen called.

"Yes. They're in the box labeled *Pans*."

"And the sugar?"

"In the box labeled *Crockery*."

There was the sound of footsteps coming up the stairs, so I quickly shoved the trunk back under the bed and stood up just in time as Jen came through the door. She was wearing jeans and an old red shirt and she looked flustered.

"Honestly," she said as pulled her long blond hair out of its clip, shook it loose, then scraped it back up again. "Your filing system needs a code breaker."

"I know where everything is," I said, and positioned myself so that my legs were in front of the bunk beds and so she couldn't see Mum's trunk.

"Well, thank God one of us does," she said as she began to poke around in the wardrobe and in the drawers. "Everything gone from in here?"

I nodded and tried to usher her out. "All downstairs. There's just some bedding, which I will pack up. And later Dad needs to disassemble the bunk beds ready for the truck and then—hurrah hurrah—later reassemble them in the new bedrooms, but as two single *separate* beds."

Jen put her arm around me and gave me a squeeze. "It's about time you had your own room, Cat. Any ideas about decorating it yet?"

"I change my mind every day."

"I'm like that about the wedding . . ."

"What! You mean about marrying Dad?"

Jen laughed. "*No*. Not about marrying him. Nothing could change my mind about that. No, I meant about what to wear. Finalizing the flowers, the details of the reception. Oh God, just thinking about it makes me panic. I've hardly done anything and it's going to be upon us before we know it. I've been so busy planning the move that everything else has gone on the back burner."

"My friend Lucy is a dress designer," I said. "And she has fab taste. When we go up to look for the dresses, maybe we could take her along?"

"Sure," said Jen. "That would be good, because we're going to have to get it all settled on that one trip."

It had long been decided that we'd go to London to buy Jen's dress, shoes, and whatever else, as there is so much more choice in the stores up there. We were also going to look at bridesmaid's clothes for me. Emma already had her outfit—she got it in Plymouth last week when she went shopping with Jen. It was mad, but totally Emma: a bright-pink fairy outfit, complete with silver wings and tiara. She looked so cute in it and wanted to wear it all the time, but Jen said not until the big day.

I wished I'd been able to find something in Plymouth as I had mixed feelings about going up to London. One part of me felt thrilled, as it's the Big City, but another part felt apprehensive because of the trouble there in past years. I'd tried to talk to Dad about it, but he told me not to be ridiculous and that we mustn't give in to terrorist threats. He was probably right. A trip up to London would be fun, and TJ had already said I could stay with her, and also, if there was time, I could meet up with Jamie. He's a mate of Lia's brother, Ollie, and is the boy I hooked up with on the recent birthday treat trip to Morocco. It was Mrs. Axford's fortieth birthday and Mr. Axford flew a bunch of us over for a long weekend. It was the trip of a lifetime for me, because I'd never flown and never been farther than London before, plus we stayed in an unbelievably fabtastic place. I'd loved every second of it and it was made all the more special by spending time with Jamie. Ollie wasn't very pleased, as he thought he had a claim on me just because we had hung out a few times when he was down from his boarding school in London. However, a few weeks before the trip, I found out that up in London he had also been seeing TJ. Neither of us knew about each other until we met. Anyway, after that, I didn't feel that I owed him anything. No doubt, he is one of the best-looking boys I've ever met and he can be fun, but he's a player. I'd always known that he was not one to get emotionally attached to or else I'd end up with a broken heart. Jamie, on the other hand, was a sweetie. Okay, not as handsome as Ollie, but he was cute in his own way and made me laugh. He'd been e-mailing me regularly since the trip, and in each e-mail he said that he wanted to see me again. That was one of the things I liked about him. He came out and said what he meant. No games or trying to be cool.

Jen glanced out of the window and then at her watch. "Oh, Lord. Here's the removal van already. Oh, God. Here we go. Come on, Cat, you'd better come down and help us load up."

The rest of the morning was spent carrying cases, boxes, and bags out to the van. Dad and one of his mates from the village helped the removal men carry furniture and heavier items, and soon the first load was ready to go.

"Right, Cat," said Dad as he slammed the back doors of the van shut. "Luke and Joe are coming with me to help unload the other end. Emma's going with Jen in her car to begin setting up the new kitchen, so you stay here, have a last look around and anything that still needs to be taken, put in the hall. Don't lift anything too heavy and I'll be back in a couple of hours to take the beds and last bits."

I watched the van chug off down the road, soon to be followed by Emma (who was wearing her bridesmaid's tiara) and Jen in her car.

As the car disappeared around the corner, I went back inside. I closed the front door behind me and the house felt eerily quiet. I went from room to room. It was weird to see them so empty: rugs rolled up, the walls bare. I wished that Dad had left a radio so at least I could have turned on some sound to fill the silence.

Having checked downstairs, I went back up and began to fold bedding from all the beds and put it in big black bin liners. When all was done and packed, there was nothing left to do but open the trunk. It was the ideal time—no one around, no disturbances—and yet I found myself hesitating. I went into what was Mum and Dad's old room, for a last look. I could still picture Mum lying in the bed in the months before she left us. She had always tried to be so cheerful although, as time went on, I could see what a strain it was on her. I crossed the room and looked out of the window down at the garden. I remembered happier times when she was well: playing with Joe in a paddling pool, squirting him with the hose pipe. Bringing out a birthday cake with candles for Luke—for me, on my birthday. I remembered her in the kitchen cooking endless meals for us. Shepherd's pie was her specialty and she made a mean apple crumble. I thought about Emma. She would have none of these memories, as she was only a baby when Mum died. No wonder she adores Jen now and follows her everywhere like a faithful puppy. But Jen *isn't* her mum.

A feeling of sudden panic came over me. We *shouldn't* be leaving this house. It was wrong. It was here that Mum had lived and been a part of our family. If we left then the already-fading memories would disappear completely. Like a painting left out in the rain: the image disintegrating into rivulets of color, then washing away to leave a blank canvas. I felt my throat tighten with emotion and tears spring to my eyes. I was afraid that I would forget my mum in the new house. The new chapter in which she didn't have a role. As I looked around the room that had once been so full of her belongings, her clothes, her presence, her scent and saw only silence and emptiness, I tried to recall more memories of her. Past times I could take with me into the future—but they wouldn't come. I couldn't even remember the sound of her voice anymore.

At that moment, the phone ringing broke the silence. I ran downstairs and picked up the receiver.

"Hey," said Lucy's voice. "Just calling to say good luck with the move."

"Oh right . . . thanks."

"Hey, you okay, Cat?" asked Lucy. "You sound— dunno . . ."

"Yeah, I'm okay . . . sort of . . . well, maybe not . . ."

"I *knew* something was up. I can tell by your voice. Come on. Tell Auntie Lucy."

"Oh nothing. It's just everyone's gone on to the new house, and I'm here doing a last bit of tidying, and it's weird being here in the empty house, and I'm wondering if we should even be moving at all, as this was where my mum lived . . . And, well, there's still that trunk—you know, my mum's one—and I found the key to it, but now I can't bring myself to open it."

"Why not?"

"There might be stuff in there I'm not meant to see. Private stuff. Dunno." It sounded lame when I said it out loud.

"Ah, but you promised to let us know what was in it," said Lucy. "Remember our Truth, Dare game?"

"I know. I will. Sometime . . . just not yet."

"Just go and do it, Cat. Do what Izzie is always saying: Feel the fear and do it anyway. What have you got to lose? It's not like you're going to find a skeleton in there."

"Oh thanks a *lot*." I laughed. "Like I'm not feel-ing spooked out enough as it is, being here with everything gone."

"Just go and do it," said Lucy, "and I'll call later to make sure that you have."

"I thought Nesta was the bossy one," I said.

"She is," said Lucy. "Just think yourself lucky it wasn't her that called. Seriously though, it will be okay. Like for me, I'd been dreading this week for ages. Not wanting to think about it. It's the week that my boyfriend, Tony—you know, Nesta's brother—gets his A-level results. He's such a brain and was offered a place at Oxford if he got good results. I knew he would, we all did, and he got the results last week: As in everything, so he'll be off there in October. A new start. We'll both be going different ways . . ."

"Oh Lucy, I'm so sorry. There's me going on and you must be gutted."

"Actually I'm okay. I knew it was coming and it's probably a good thing that he's going. We drive each other and everyone around us mad with our strange on-off relationship."

"But Oxford's not far. You can still see him."

"'Course. And he'll be home in the holidays—but we decided no commitments, no promises that we know we won't keep. I mean, hey, last thing I want to be is a stone around his neck. No. But we did make a pact. If we both have got to thirty and are still unattached, then we'll get back together."

"Thirty! But that's a million years away. Anything could happen."

"Exactly. Be fun. And you know what? It feels okay. I have to let him go. And with the pact, it doesn't feel totally final, if you know what I mean. I'll see him in the holidays, yeah, I'll maybe even hear that he's fallen in love, but I can always tell myself: Ah, but there's always when we're thirty!"

"He's older than you, so when *he's* thirty or *you* are?"

"When he is," said Lucy.

"Wow. I think that is so cool. It sounds like the beginning of a movie."

"Yeah," said Lucy. "Exciting, huh? As you said, anything might happen so feel the fear and do it anyway."

"Hey, what about the other boys? How did they do?" I asked as I knew that Nesta's boyfriend, William, and TJ's boyfriend, Luke, and Lucy's brother, Steve, had also been doing their A-levels.

"They all did good. William is going to university here in London so Nesta is well chuffed about that. Luke is going to drama school and also staying in London so TJ is made up about that as well. Steve has got a place in Bristol so he'll be moving away. All change, huh?"

"I guess," I said, and made a mental note to let Becca know about Steve, that is if she didn't already. Like Jamie and me, they keep in touch by e-mail. Bristol isn't too far from where we live so maybe they could continue their relationship.

After I'd put the phone down, I took a deep breath and looked up the stairs. Feel the fear and do it anyway, Lucy had said. Be brave, Mum'd said in the letter that she'd left me. Always be brave.

I turned on my heel, went back up the stairs, into my room, pulled the trunk out from under the bed, put the key in the lock, and opened it.

I was immediately hit with a sweet woody scent. I know that smell, I thought. It's patchouli. I knew exactly what it was, because Izzie wore it and had told me that it was an essential oil used in aromatherapy and that the oil was extracted from tree bark. How strange that Mum had known about it. I peered into the open trunk and slowly and carefully began to take out what I found in there. Bits of paper, articles torn out from papers and magazines, and a photo album, which I opened immediately. I could hardly believe my eyes. I thought I knew every photograph that we had of Mum and yet here were pages more. Pages charting her life. Mum as a little girl, holding her mother's hand. On a bike looking about seven. Mum as a teenager with various hairstyles: long hair, short, big hair. Wearing big shoulder pads. One of her in a cap and gown receiving a degree, and then there was Dad looking so young and handsome. Both of them crammed into a photo booth making goofy faces. And then one in a hospital bed holding a baby, her eyes shining. Me. I must have barely been born.

I lost all track of time as I sat on the floor and pored over the wealth of treasures in the trunk. As well as the photo album, there was a small soap bag containing the oil that smelled so strongly. There were three tiny bottles labeled *sandalwood, patchouli,* and *jasmine*. A couple of slides of someone I didn't know. A man standing on a beach with his back to the camera. He was naked! Who was that? I wondered. Not Dad. He's not that tall. Maybe an early boyfriend from pre-Dad days. There were bits and pieces from my childhood, awful splotches of paintings I had done and signed: Cat Kennedy. Same from Luke. She had kept them all. A couple of Mother's Day cards. Valentines from Dad. A tiny crystal swan. A couple of Oriental-looking bookmarks. The words to a song written by Bob Dylan. A file that appeared to be full of bank statements and old household bills.

At the bottom of the trunk was a book with a gold latch on it, but it wasn't locked. I flicked open the cover and there was a drawing on the first page in green ink of a skull and crossbones and the words *PRIVATE PROPERTY.* And then a date. I quickly did the math. Almost twenty years ago. Unbelievable. It was a diary from when Mum was a teenager. Private property. I oughtn't to be reading this, I thought as another file caught my eye. I put the diary aside and flipped the file open.

It was stuffed with photos and notes, as if Mum had been doing a project or essay. I glanced over the photos—some were of landscapes and exotic skies. And then there was Mum again, this time as a young woman. Before Dad, I think. She was tanned with sun-kissed hair, smiling into the camera. Another of her at an airport with a rucksack slung over her shoulder. Ohmigod. It was Marrakech. I could see the name of the airport in the background of the photo. So Mum had been to Morocco as well. Maybe we even went to some of the same places, I thought as I began to read her notes. How amazing.

I was so absorbed that I hardly noticed the sound of footsteps on the stairs.

"Cat, where are you?" called Dad.

Too late to shove anything away and the blankets to hide the trunk were packed. Dad burst into the room and looked surprised to find me kneeling on the floor. He looked even more surprised when he realized that I was surrounded by photos of Mum and her letters and papers.

"I never realized that Mum spent time in Morocco?" I said as his face went white and he sank to his knees to join me in looking through what was left of his wife. My mum.

"**YOUR MATES ARE HERE,**" said Jen as soon as Dad and I drew up in front of the new house. She jerked her thumb inside. "Becca and Lia are in the kitchen."

I was just about to dash inside when a second van drew up outside.

"Number fourteen?" asked the driver, looking at Dad.

Dad looked puzzled. "Yes," he said. "But the van we booked has already been and gone. Sure you got the right place?"

"Says number fourteen on the delivery note," said the man as he got out, opened the back of his van, reached in, and brought out an enormous bouquet of white roses. He saw Jen at the front door so took them over to her.

She glanced over at Dad and her cheeks turned

rosy with pleasure. "Thank you," she said as she looked for the card and Becca and Lia appeared from inside and ooh-ed and ah-ed over the flowers. Jen looked over at Dad. "Oh, but you shouldn't have."

Dad looked like he was going to panic. "But, I *didn't*," he whispered to me. "Oh dear . . ."

"Oh! They're not for me," said Jen with a light laugh, as she read the card then held the bouquet out to me. "Cat, they're for you."

"For me!"

"Wow," said Becca. "Who are they from? They look like they cost a fortune."

I took the card from Jen and read it.

To Cat.
This is the first time I have bought flowers for a girl. White roses to say I think that you're special. Wishing you many happy times in your new home. Love Jamie.

"They're from Jamie," I said.

"Oh, that's so sweet," said Lia. "And so typical of him. He's so thoughtful."

"Waste of blooming money," said Luke as he went past. "What you supposed to do with them? Can't eat them."

I was so touched that I tried to call Jamie on his mobile straight away, but his voicemail was on. No one had ever bought me flowers before and they were a stunning bunch. I felt a warm glow spread through me and it felt so good after my melancholy morning at the old house. The flowers were a good omen. This was going to be a good new chapter.

I left Dad mumbling to Jen about how he was sorry that he hadn't thought of a gesture like flowers to welcome her, and she was trying to reassure him that it didn't matter, although I think she was disappointed that they weren't for her. Suddenly Dad lifted her up into his arms.

"Better carry you over the threshold then, hadn't I?" he asked, and she laughed as he began to walk up the steps. "Oh . . . bla . . . arrrgh . . ." Dad staggered back, gasped in pain, and dropped Jen on the lawn. "Oh—my back . . . It's gone." He couldn't stand up straight and hobbled like a bent old man into the hall, where he put a hand out to the banister and groaned with pain. Jen leaped up and followed after him.

"Are you okay? Are you okay?" she asked.

Dad let out a moan so she led him into the kitchen and made him sit down.

"Hmm," I said with a grin. "Interesting start."

"Interesting start!" said Lia. "Aren't you worried about him?"

"He'll be okay. His back always locks when he lifts heavy things. Not that Jen is that heavy, but all the same, he should know better. He's got exercises to do to crick it back. Hey, let's explore."

Becca and Lia looked at my dad, then at me, then shrugged. They might think I was being unsympathetic, but I knew he'd be all right. He'd cricked his back a thousand times lifting stuff for the shop and we knew he didn't like us to make a fuss.

I couldn't wait to look around properly, as I'd only been to the house once—and that was under the beady eye of the real estate agent—so I hadn't really been able to get the feel of the place. It was semi-detached and I think I'd heard Dad say that it was built in the 1950s. At the front was a small garden and path leading to the porch and entrance. On the ground floor was a large reception room that went from the front of the house all the way to French windows at the back. I think it must have been two rooms once, but someone had knocked them through into one, giving the room a lovely feeling of space. To the left was an airy kitchen-diner, outside a long narrow garden with apple and cherry trees at the end.

"You all right, Mr. Kennedy?" Lia asked when we went into the kitchen, where Jen was searching in the unpacked boxes for painkillers while Dad lay groaning on the kitchen table. He weakly gave her the thumbs-up as I put my flowers in some water in the sink.

"Have you seen my room?" I asked, and when they shook their heads, I led them upstairs.

My bedroom was fab. Like the rest of the house, it was light and spacious with a built-in wardrobe area. And I knew exactly where I was going to have the bed: along the wall by the window, so that some days, I could sit and look out at the back garden and fields beyond.

"Fantabeedosiedobeetabulous," I said as I envisaged how it was going to look and the feeling of space I was going to have. In the last place I had the top bunk, so if I sat up in bed, my head almost touched the ceiling. "I can't believe this. It's sooooo perfect. The whole place is fab, fab, fab."

At that moment, there was a crash then a moan in the hall. We ran to see what had happened.

"Help . . . *Help* . . ." whimpered a boy's voice.

It sounded like Joe.

"Joe? Is that you? Where are you?" asked Becca.

"Up here."

"Up where?" I asked and looked up.

Becca and Lia burst out laughing, for right in the middle of the ceiling, exactly where a lightbulb should be hanging, was Joe's left leg. It had come through the ceiling.

"Joe, what happened?" I called up.

"I fell off one of the joists," he said. "Help

me before the rest of me comes through."

"Hmm, looking for a job as a light shade?" asked Becca.

"Not funny," whimpered Joe. "I'm stuck."

"I'll get Dad," I said, and was about to head off downstairs.

"No," cried Joe from above. "He'll kill me."

We ran up to the second floor and into Joe's new bedroom, but I couldn't see him. "Where are you? What happened?"

"In here," said Joe. "I'm in the dummy attic."

"There," said Becca as she pointed at a small knee-high door on the wall to our right and went over to kneel down by it. Lia and I went with her and, indeed, the door led to an area in the roof. In the space between two of the joists was a very miserable-looking Joe.

"I was having a look around and balancing on one of the beams," he sniveled, "when I slipped and my leg went through the ceiling."

"It's only plaster," I said. "It's not meant to be walked on."

"D'oh, I know that," groaned Joe. "Least I do now. Come on, I'm a celebrity, get me out of here."

"I'll get him," said Becca, and she squeezed in and gently hauled Joe up, back on to a beam, then pulled him back into his room. His face was tear-stained and my heart went straight out to him.

"Hey, it's okay," I said. "You're okay. You're safe now. Were you scared that you were going to fall?"

"Yes . . . and . . . but . . . I . . . I've ruined the new house and I've only been in it for five minutes. Dad's going to hate me and think I'm stupid and—"

I put my arms round him and let him sob for a moment. Dear Joe. So often acting the tough guy, so determined to grow up so fast, but at times like this, it was clear he was vulnerable underneath all the bravado.

"Hey, hey. It's going to be okay," I said. "We won't tell Dad today and chances are he won't even notice for weeks, if ever. I mean who looks up when they're going down the corridor? Don't worry. We can maybe even try and get Squidge in to fix it. He's a dab hand at DIY."

"Do you think?" He sniffed.

"Yeah. It's going to be great here. Don't you worry. Just great," I said.

I couldn't have been more mistaken. For the rest of the day, everything that could go wrong, did.

Dad, having recovered from his back lock, was nailing something up in the kitchen and hit a water pipe in the wall. Water came gushing out—unfortunately just as Emma was passing by, so she got an unexpected shower and didn't like that one bit. And then we had to call for an emergency plumber, which Dad didn't like because of the expense.

The beds arrived in their dismantled state, but no one could find the bag with the tools so Dad couldn't put them together.

And Emma was prancing around in the living room and tripped and pulled out the main phone socket so that we couldn't get a dial tone. When we called on the mobile to try and get someone out, they said that a technician wouldn't be available until Tuesday.

So much for my good omen, I thought as I wondered what was going to go wrong next.

For a couple of hours things went peacefully enough, and we emptied endless boxes and bags and began to put things away.

Dad drove into the village to get fish and chips for supper, drop Becca and Lia home, and borrow a toolbox to put the beds together.

In the meantime, the light was beginning to fade and, after a busy day, I was looking forward to a good night's sleep in my new room. However, unbeknownst to the rest of us, Luke was upstairs attempting to wire up the computer and printer, and somehow managed to fuse all the lights in the house. Of course, it being a new house, no one had thought to look where the fuse box was, and the situation fast turned to farce as we scrabbled around in the dark trying to find it. Not an easy task with no lights—and no candles either, because no one could remember which box they had been packed into. Luckily, I remembered that I had one of my lovely smelly ones that I'd bought in Morocco in one of my cases, and Joe found a small torch in his rucksack, so we all convened in the living room to try and decide what to do next.

That was when Dad arrived back with the fish and chips. He was great about it and made us all sit in the kitchen round the table with my candle on it. We had to eat from the paper with our fingers, though, as no one knew where the plates or knives and forks were either.

"This is great," he said. "Our first supper in the new house. We're warm. We've got food. We'll get everything else sorted in the morning."

"But where are the kids going to sleep?" asked Jen. "We have our bed, but the others need putting back together."

"We can sleep on the floor," said Joe, who was still worried about getting a telling off when the hole in the ceiling was discovered. "It will be like camping, only indoors."

"That's my boy," said Dad.

"But I'm bored," said Emma. "I want to watch my cartoons and . . . I don't like the dark."

I was about to lean over and get her to come and sit on my knee when she got up and went to Jen.

"We can tell stories," said Jen as she gave Emma a cuddle. "Or sing some songs."

"Don't want to," said Emma. "I'm scared."

"Yeah, the place might be haunted," said Joe. "Wuhoooooooo. Yeah, I bet there are ghosts right now looking in through the window, watching us, waiting . . ."

"Now stop that, Joe," said Dad.

"Yeah," said Luke. "Ghosts who really like little girls to eat . . ."

"Luke!" said Dad.

Emma, who is easy to scare, looked freaked as she stared at the dark window. "This house might be haunted," she wailed. "We can't stay here."

"It's not haunted," said Jen. "I promise you."

"Cat, draw the curtains," said Dad.

I got up to draw the curtains. Only there weren't any. "Er, slight problem, Dad," I said, and everyone burst out laughing when they realized.

So much for the fab new start, I thought as I went back to my place at the table with the others.

No light. No phone. No curtains. No electricity and no one knew where anything was.

It was then that I got the giggles. "New chapter, hey, Jen?"

"Ah," she replied. "Well that's the thing about new chapters, nobody knows exactly what's in them . . ."

6   Reality Kicks In

THE CHURCH DOOR OPENED. An usher released a basket of white doves, another let go of fifty white balloons, and a hundred guests turned to look at me as an orchestra of violins began to play. Everyone ooh-ed and ah-ed as I began to walk up the aisle with Becca and Lia behind me as my bridesmaids. Waiting at the altar for me with a white rose in his hand was Jamie. As I reached him, he smiled into my eyes and leaned down to ki—

"Whose boots are these on the floor?" Jen yelled up the stairs. "And *who* has left this T-shirt on the banister when it belongs in the laundry basket?"

My snog reverie about Jamie was further shattered by the sound of a door slamming down below and footsteps coming up the stairs. I got up from my bed and went out to the corridor to see Luke with the offending T-shirt in hand. He was about to go into the bathroom, and rolled his eyes when he saw me.

"Honestly," he said as he threw the T-shirt into the basket. "I wish she'd chill! It's not even as if it's term time."

"She's just not used to us," I said, although I had been feeling the same way as Luke in the last few days since we moved in. Living with Jen was like having a very strict teacher come to stay. Do this, don't do that. Up until now, she'd only stayed at our house for the occasional night and sometimes the weekend. She'd never lived with us permanently before so we'd never got a true impression of what she was like.

On one hand, life in the new house was beginning to feel more normal as the electricity went back on, things were unpacked and put away, and our daily routine began to be established again. On the other hand, it was slowly becoming clear that Jen liked things to be done a certain way. Her way.

"You can't be serious," I heard her say as I went downstairs. "You're not putting that up in my living room."

"Er . . . *our* living room," said Dad.

"That's what I meant. Sorry. Sorry," said Jen as I entered the room in time to see her taking down an oil painting of a landscape that had been up in the other house as far back as I can remember. "But . . . I mean, it *is* hideous."

"Is it? I rather liked it," said Dad. "But you know I haven't got a clue when it comes to art. What do you think, Cat?"

I had never liked the painting either, but it seemed that more and more of Jen's stuff was on display and more and more of ours wasn"t. "Um . . . Oh, I don't know," I said. "I know it's a bit naff, but it would be good to have a couple of things up to remind us of the old house."

"Where did it come from?" asked Jen. "A junk shop?"

"Um . . . it was a wedding present, I think," said Dad. "From Laura's aunt Dora."

Jen immediately looked embarrassed. "A wedding present? Oh! In that case . . . I would never ask you to throw out anything that has sentimental value, anything that belonged to your wife. You know that, don't you? Oh God, now I feel like I've been so insensitive."

Dad put his arm around her. "Come to think of it, Laura never liked that painting either, but was always worried that Dora would turn up and demand to know where it was. Dora's passed away too now, so if you hate it, then it goes."

Hmm, this is going to be interesting, I thought as I went into the kitchen. I had been to Jen's flat over in Plymouth before she sold it. It was nice, but she obviously favored a very different style in décor to Dad. Jen's style was clean, simple, and modern. Dad's style, if you could even call it a style, was comfy clutter. Our furniture was a real mess, with wobbly legs glued back on, scratched surfaces, rips and tears in old chairs—make-do stuff that no one else wanted. It was strange because, until I saw our bits and pieces in the "to be chucked" pile, I hadn't realized how attached I was to them. They were like old friends—emphasis being on the word "old." Ah well, I thought as I grabbed a piece of toast from the kitchen table and headed back up to my room, I will leave them to get on with it. Maybe we should all move forward, and as long as Jen didn't start telling me what to do in my room and didn't go poking around in the trunk of Mum's stuff that I had found, I didn't care.

I'd hidden the trunk under my bed and even though Dad knew it was there, he seemed only too relieved to hand the responsibility for it over to me. I guessed that it was hard for him to have something so personal of Mum's turn up at a time like this—a time when he was about to get married to another woman. I tried to get him to talk about it, but I should have known better; Dad's way of dealing with difficult or painful emotions was to shut them out and pretend that they weren't there. Like the day he had found me in the old house looking through the trunk. I would have thought that he'd have been interested, but he only gave the things a cursory glance. Maybe it was too raw for him still, even after six years. I tried to understand and respect his way of doing things, but I couldn't help but wonder if part of him felt like I did, guilty for moving on and leaving Mum behind.

Luke and Joe had taken Emma out to the village

so I knew that I had some time alone to look at the diary in the trunk. I'd been dying to look at it properly, although when I'd first found it, I felt I shouldn't be looking at it at all. However, as the days had gone by, my curiosity had begun to get the better of me. Strange turn of events, I thought as I pulled the diary out and sat on the bed with it. It should be her finding my diary and feeling that she was intruding, not this way round.

I turned the page and began to read . . . and read . . .

"So how's it going with the lovebirds?" asked Becca later in the day, when I met her down by Kingsand Bay to get ice cream.

"What, me and Jamie?" I said as I bought two vanilla cones and we went to sit on the bench overlooking the bay. "Looks like I might be seeing him soon, at least I hope I will."

"Actually I meant with your dad and Jen, but first things first, how come you'll be seeing Jamie?"

"Jen said that I could stay an extra day with TJ after we've been wedding shopping, and come back on the train, so I'm going to go and see him then. I haven't managed to tell him yet, although I've been calling and calling but I keep getting his voicemail or the machine at his house. I also sent him a text message in the hope he'd pick that up. I hope he'll be pleased to see me and hasn't gone off me."

"Why would he go off you, idiot? He wouldn't have sent the flowers if he'd lost interest."

"I guess. I just wish I could get through."

"You could surprise him," said Becca. "Find out from Ollie where he might be, like a café or somewhere he hangs out, and then just casually walk by. It will blow his mind and he'll be so knocked out to see you."

"Hey, good idea," I said. "Jamie likes surprises, but no way will Ollie tell me where he is. He was well peeved that I dropped him for Jamie."

"I'll find out then."

"You? How?"

Becca tapped the side of her nose. "Easy. I'll find out from Lia."

"Cool," I said.

"And how are the other lovebirds? The old ones?

Your dad and Jen? Are they happy in their new love nest?"

"Oh, them . . ." As we ate our ice creams, I filled Becca in on the situation. "They're like total opposites, and I so hope that they don't fall out before they even get married. It's made me think that maybe it's not a good idea to live with some-one before a wedding, because they get to know all your annoying habits and moods and stuff. If you haven't lived with them then you can still fool them into thinking that you're cool and in a good mood and look fab all the time. Like Jen always used to look immaculate, but now I've seen her with her hair a mess and no makeup on in the morning and getting cross. If it's been a shock for me, imagine how Dad feels."

"He won't even notice," said Becca. "He's smitten."

"I'm not so sure anymore. Like Dad's an early-morning person, up with the larks with loads of energy. Jen is a late-night bird and has told us all that we're not to talk to her until at least ten, when she's had minimum two cups of coffee. He likes the radio on in the morning. She switches it off the moment she goes downstairs. She likes silence until the evening and *then* she turns into Mrs Sociable, let's have the whole world round. She has millions of friends. They've been coming round by the carload to inspect the house. Dad, as you know, doesn't have any friends. Between the shop and looking after the four of us, he never had any time. Jen loves a house full of people, the more the merrier. By the evening, Dad has wound down and likes it quiet. And she hates him smoking. He has to go and stand out in the garden to smoke one of his rollies. I don't think he had a clue what he was letting himself in for. God help them if they ever make it to the altar."

"Nah," said Becca. "Opposites attract."

"Maybe. But all the more reason not to spend too much time together then. In fact, I don't understand the need to live together, myself. I've been thinking about weddings a lot lately with Jen and Dad's coming up, and am beginning to think that I may never get married. I mean, yeah, I'd like the dress and the ceremony and getting the presents and that—but having to live with someone . . . Like, why? If you have a choice, what on earth for? I have had to spend so many years sharing a room with Emma, plus the wardrobe and even sharing the bunk beds, and finally, *finally*, I get my own room with my own drawers and cupboard space, why would I want to share it with someone again? Ever? And if you get married you have to share your bed. *Why?* Seems mad to me, if you can afford to have two beds. If I do ever get married—and I think I've decided today that I probably never will—I would insist that we had separate beds, if not separate rooms, if not separate houses. Maybe live next door to each other."

Becca laughed. "You old romantic, you. Isn't it obvious why people want to share a room and a bed?"

"No."

"To snog each other, dummy. And get naked and stuff . . . you know."

"Yeah, okay, but you could do that anywhere. Why not get that over with, and then luxuriate in your own space and bed without someone cramping you. I loooove having my own bed now. I've sprayed the sheets with perfume and Jen gave me some pretty white lace pillowcases. If some boy got in there with smelly feet and messed it all up, I'm afraid I'd have to kick him out."

Becca rolled her eyes. "God help whoever you end up married to! How are the boys taking it?"

"Don't like being told what to do. I know I used to boss them around, but they could talk back to me. They don't feel they can with Jen. And when it comes to telly, I think we're going to have some major battles before the week is out. Dad likes documentaries. Jen likes the soaps. The boys like all the sci-fi and adventure films. Emma likes the cartoons. And I, when I can get in at all, like MTV and romcom films. Another reason not to get married. If you're single, you get the remote. That would be heaven to me: one evening watching what *I* want on telly for a change."

"You can always come to my house, if that's all you want," said Becca. "We can watch the telly in my room or we can go up to Lia's——"

"And watch a different telly every ten minutes," I interrupted.

Becca laughed. There were about fifteen televisions up at the Axfords'. One in every guest room and others dotted around other parts of the house.

"But Emma," said Becca, "I bet she loves having Jen."

I nodded. I felt weird about that and was still getting my head around it. It was like I had been shoved out of the picture as far as being anyone's substitute mum went, and although that was exactly what I wanted in one way, in another I felt unwanted. I was so used to being the one that Emma ran to for a cuddle or to tell her news. Now it was Jen, Jen, Jen. She wasn't our mother. But then again, Emma had never known our mum. She probably couldn't even remember her at all.

"Honestly, though," I sighed, "it's not exactly how I thought it would be. I thought Jen and I were going to be like mates, but now I'm not so sure. I mean it's good and everything . . . just . . . I guess it's going to take some getting used to, that's all."

Becca nodded. "For me, too."

I squeezed her arm in sympathy. Becca had been going through a hard time lately as her mum and dad had just separated. Although they were going to stay friends and her dad wasn't moving too far away, I knew that Becca was having to do some readjusting, too.

"Funny, isn't it?" I said. "You're getting used to having one less person around. We're getting used to having one more around."

Becca nodded. "Think it's always going to be like this—life? Everything always changing? Nothing staying the same?"

"Yep," I replied, and then chucked my cone over the wall, where it was instantly swooped upon by a seagull. "Except ice cream being good. That stays the same."

London

"I'M NEVER GOING TO find anything," Jen sighed, after she'd tried on what seemed like the hundredth wedding dress. "I'm exhausted."

She wasn't the only one. We'd been up since the crack of dawn. Dad had dropped us in Plymouth and we'd caught the six o'clock train to London Paddington. Since then we'd been to all the large department stores in Oxford Street, Regent Street, and Knightsbridge, and although a couple of the dresses we'd seen looked okay, as Jen said, "Who wants to look 'okay' on their wedding day? I want to look *sensational*."

It was fun to be in the big city and take in all the crowds and the shops, but there was still a part of me that couldn't let go and really enjoy it because I felt scared that something bad might happen. I didn't want to be a total wimp, though, especially after having spent so long reading my mum's file and diary. It seemed that she had been fearless, traveling all over the Far East, India, and Africa before she was married, and I got the impression that she had aspirations to be a travel writer. I didn't like to think that I might be letting her down by being a pathetic scaredy-cat who was afraid to even go on the Underground when she had hiked up mountains, crossed deserts, taken planes to remote countries, and gone into uncharted territory without a second thought. I liked to think that I had inherited some of her adventurous spirit.

"It's time to meet Lucy in Notting Hill," I said as I glanced at my watch. "She said she knows a great bridal shop there."

"I hope so," said Jen as she stuck her hand out into the oncoming traffic. "Let's get a cab. My feet are beginning to kill me."

A taxi driver soon saw us and stopped by the side of the road.

"Notting Hill," said Jen as we climbed in.

Inwardly, I breathed a sigh of relief. "Phew," I

said as we sat back and the driver took off. "I don't like going on the Underground."

"Too many people, huh?" asked Jen. "It can be overwhelming if you're not used to it."

"Partly," I agreed, "but also . . ." I wasn't sure whether to say anything in case she thought I was stupid.

"Also what, Cat?"

"Bombs," I admitted. "Remember a while ago there were those terrorists . . ."

Jen immediately put her arm around me. "Oh Cat. Why didn't you say?"

"Thought you might think I was being childish."

"Never," said Jen. "How do you think all us guys who work in the airlines feel, traveling the world? Believe me, we've all had our wobbly moments, too. Days when I look at *all* the passengers with suspicious eyes and think they are terrorists—even little old grannies. And not just on the airplane. Some days I'm the same on buses, Tube, trains, any crowd situation. That's the trouble. We no longer know what the enemy looks like or where they're going to strike."

"I know. And I was doing what you said just now on the Tube," I said. "Everyone looked suspicious and my imagination was running riot. So how do you deal with it?"

"Feel the fear and do it anyway."

"That's my friend Izzie's philosophy," I said.

"Good for her. Life goes on. You have to go on with it."

"That's what Dad said."

"I can imagine," said Jen. "And he's right; on the one hand, yes, terrorism is a very real threat—but on the other hand, we can't give in to them and stop going about our business. I try to be philosophical and say, if it's my time, it's my time—whether it's on a Tube or I have a heart attack or—"

"Cancer, like Mum had."

Jen nodded. "God, this is a depressing conversation we're having, for such a lovely summer's day!"

"I guess," I said, "but actually it's good to talk about this stuff to someone, and it's impossible to talk to Dad about it. He bottles everything up and shuts off if anyone brings up a difficult subject."

Jen rolled her eyes. "Tell me about it," she agreed.

"I thought a lot about death when Mum passed away. I know it's a fact. We're born, we die—we just don't know when. I do think I'd prefer to die in my bed in my sleep at a ripe old age, though, than be blown up by some mad person."

"Me too," said Jen. "Me too. But really, Cat, millions and millions of people travel on the Tube every day and on the airlines and are perfectly safe. The chances of anything happening to you are very remote. Of course that's not to say that something won't happen, but the odds are against it. I don't know. It's a strange old business, isn't it? Like my second cousin, Josie. She was on holiday in Thailand in 2004 when the tsunami hit on Boxing Day. Thank God she wasn't anywhere near the beach at the time and was okay, but you would think that there was nowhere safer, wouldn't you? White beach. Turquoise sea. Paradise. And then along came that mammoth wave and wiped out thousands."

"And all the earthquakes. It's a miracle we survive at all!"

Jen smiled a sad smile. "I know. Maybe it is. So much we don't know or understand—whether acts of man or acts of God. In the meantime though, I think the thing is to enjoy the life we have to its maximum. As you said, none of us knows when our time is going to be up so make the most of the life you've got. Have good times. Let the people you love know that you love them. All that stuff—and don't let the bad news get you down."

I gave her a hug. "I agree—and thanks. It's so easy talking to you."

"Anytime," said Jen and hugged me back.

As we drove through the busy streets of London toward Notting Hill, I felt a lot better about being there, plus I felt closer to Jen again, as if the last few days of the mad move had been wiped out and we were friends again.

I gazed out of the taxi window at the hordes of people dashing about their lives. Look at us all, I thought. So many out there, all shapes, sizes, colors, all with their own stories, hopes, goals, disappointments. And for all our twenty-first-century technology and sophistication, we don't know much at all about what it all means. But Jen's right. We should appreciate what we do have while we have it. *I* should. I made an inner resolution to make the most of my life and not waste time being moody, depressed, or mad with my mates or family.

Lucy and Izzie were waiting for us at our arranged meeting place outside the Tube station and listened sympathetically as Jen despaired about not being able to find a dress.

Lucy nodded. "I know, too many meringue-type things. They don't do much for anyone, even really slim people like you. What you want is simple, elegant, beautifully cut."

"Exactly," said Jen. "But can we find anything like that? No."

"I think I have just the place for you," said Lucy. "I come down to this area a lot looking for fabric for making my clothes and found this shop I think you're going to love. If I ever get married, I'd get something from there."

Jen grinned back at her. "Lead the way," she said.

The shop was on a side road off Portobello Road

and it specialized in vintage wedding clothes. The middle-aged blond lady who ran it introduced herself as Nicola and treated us like her best friends. She laid on coffee, tea, soft drinks, scones, *and* Belgian chocolates and she made it great fun deciding what look to go for.

"Your wedding is such a special time," she said, "and I like to make picking the outfit part of that rather than it being a chore."

Nothing was too much trouble for her and, after three hours trying on just about every item of clothing in there, Jen had the most exquisite outfit sorted. It was exactly what Lucy had described. Simple and elegant—a slip of a dress in fine ivory silk that was cut on the bias. Over the dress was a three-quarter-length antique lace jacket with hand-beading round the edges. It was so delicate and made Jen look like an Edwardian princess. The lady who owned the shop advised Jen to put her hair up on the day and not to wear a veil but instead to wear a handmade tiara. She found her the most gorgeous one, made of tiny gold fabric leaves, sea pearls, and lace flowers—the sort of thing that you would imagine the Queen of the Fairies would wear.

We also found a dress for me. It was so easy shopping with Nicola. She would pull a couple of things out and they would be perfect. Like Jen's, the dress we settled on was simple: no sleeves, scooped low at the back, and made from fine silk in pale blue. I felt amazing in it. Like a million dollars.

"If you send it up to me after the wedding," said Lucy, "I'll shorten it for you as it would make a really hot party dress."

"Right," said Jen, after she'd handed over her credit card and everything was paid for. "Who's for a cruise down Portobello Road before I get the train back? Are you sure you want to stay an extra day, Cat? You can come back with me if you like."

I knew she was giving me a get-out clause in case I still felt anxious, but my earlier fear seemed to have evaporated since our talk, plus I realized that Lucy and her mates used the Tube no problem. I wasn't going to miss out on spending more time with them just because I had an overactive imagination.

"You can't go back,' said Lucy. "We've got it all planned for this evening. DVD and sleepover at TJ's."

"Up to you, Cat," said Jen.

"I'll stay." I grinned back at her. I was finding out fast that with good mates to hang out with, life in the city could be fun after all.

Boys!

"DOESN'T LOVERBOY JAMIE live round here some-where?" asked Izzie, after we had seen Jen off in a cab to go back to the station to catch her train.

"Holland Park," I said. "I've been trying to ring him, but I keep getting the answering machine at his house and the voice service on his mobile, and there's no reply to the text message I left him either."

"I thought you guys e-mailed?" said Lucy.

"We do. Did. But Luke did something to our computer when setting it up at the new house and we haven't been able to get or send e-mail. There might be a whole pile from him waiting, for all I know—either that or he's moved on."

"From a babe like you? No way," said Lucy. "There's probably some reason and he'll tell you when he sees you."

"Hope so," I said.

"Holland Park's just down the road," said Izzie, pointing down off in the distance.

"Have you set up a date to see him while you're up here?" asked Lucy.

I shook my head. "Becca said I should surprise him, but I'm not so sure about that – which is why I've been trying to ring him. I mean, I know *I'd* like some warning . . ."

"We *could* surprise him," said Lucy. "We're so close. Oh, let's. I'm dying to see what he looks like. What's the address?"

I scrabbled around in my bag and pulled out my purse with the scrap of paper that I'd written Jamie's details on. I showed it to Izzie.

"I know exactly where this is," she said setting off along the pavement. "Come on. Mission: Find Jamie."

"But what are we going to do? We can't just go up to his house and ring the bell."

"Oh yes we can," chorused Lucy and Izzie.

Ten minutes later, we found ourselves on a wide road not far from Holland Park Tube station. The houses were awesome. Grand ivory villas that resembled hotels more than houses. He can't possibly live in one of these, I thought as we looked at the numbers as we went along.

Lucy stopped in front of a gate between two white pillars. "Number twenty-three," she said as she looked at a brass plate. "This is it."

I glanced up the path at the five-story town house towering in front of us, and felt very small. "I'm not going in there," I said. "It's . . . so *posh*. Jamie never said that his family was loaded or anything."

"So what if he's posh?" said Lucy. "You're not a peasant." She laughed and began to talk in a thick country-yokel accent. "Oo-ar, Jamie mi lord, me be a simple country maiden not worthy of speaking to the likes of posh folks like you. I be from Cornwall, where we only just got electricity."

I laughed, but actually that was exactly how I felt—like a country yokel.

"I can't believe you'd feel, like, intimidated when one of your best friends is Lia Axford—and you don't get posher than their house," said Izzie. "You feel at home there, don't you?"

"Yeah, I do . . ." I couldn't explain why I felt the way I did. It was true, the Axfords' place was mega, but it was also friendly and lived in. Jamie's house looked cold and imposing.

"I used to feel I didn't belong in nobby places," said Lucy, "like those posh boutiques where mannequin-type assistants look at you like you've crawled in from under a rock, or hotels where receptionists look you up and down as if to say, 'And what do you think you're doing here, you splodge of insignificant nothingness?' And then Nesta said this thing to me— that no one can make you feel inferior without your permission, and I thought: yeah, right. Nobody knows who I am or anything about me, I might be über-rich for all they know. I might be a Russian princess or the daughter of a millionaire. Whatever. I belong in those shops and hotels as much as anybody and I'm not going to let anyone scare me off by looking down their snobby stuck-up noses."

I couldn't help but laugh as Lucy made her speech with such an earnest expression on her face. There clearly had been a time she had been intimidated and she had had to make her way through it.

"Must be worth about five million," Izzie pronounced as she opened the gate and looked up at the house. "I know because Nesta used to have a boyfriend who lived round here. Simon Peddington Lee. His family were stonkingly rich."

"Oh let's come back another time," I said as I pulled back. "I can't face seeing Jamie just now."

Izzie, however, was already at the front door and had rung the bell.

I was about to go and hide behind a bush in the front garden when I thought, oh don't be so stupid, Cat. This is Jamie. Jamie who likes me. What am I so afraid of? He'd think I was a right dope if he opened the door and found me hiding behind a privet bush.

Izzie bent over and looked through the letter box. "Looks like no one's home," she said as she straightened up and rang the bell again.

We waited a few more minutes, but all was silence within. I breathed a sigh of relief as Izzie and Lucy decided to give up.

"Let's go to High Street Kensington," said Lucy. "There are some fab shops there, then we can go into a department store and try on all the perfumes."

We walked down a few streets full of similar houses to Jamie's and soon found ourselves on a street lined with interesting shops full of the most awesome things—antiques, old mirrors as big as a wall, beautiful statues, light-fittings, heavy brocade fabrics—and then a row of gorgeous-looking boutiques full of clothes that looked like they were made for princesses. I felt in awe not only by the style, but by the prices—like four hundred pounds for a top and two hundred pounds for a pair of shoes.

Izzie and Lucy were gazing in a shoe shop window when I saw him. Jamie. He was in a florist's opposite and, by the look of it, he was buying a huge bunch of white roses.

"Oh God," I cried, and darted into the shop porch and turned my face away from the street in case he saw me. I felt like someone had plunged a knife into my stomach. White roses. They were the flowers he had sent me. The first flowers he had bought for a girl, he had said. Yeah right, looks like it, I thought as I took a peek and watched Jamie hand over some cash.

"What? Who?" asked Lucy as she looked up from the window she'd been absorbed in.

"Jamie. He's in that florist's," I said, and pointed to the shop.

"But that's brilliant," said Izzie. "We can go in and surprise him."

"Nooooooo," I objected. "You don't understand. He's buying white roses."

"So?" asked Lucy.

"Those are the flowers he bought for me. I thought they were special, just for me, but he has clearly got someone up here to give them to."

"You don't know that," said Lucy. "Is he the guy in the jeans and grey hoodie?"

I poked my head out. "Yes. What's he doing now?"

"He's just come out of the shop. He's turned left and is walking away from us toward—oh! Oh dear . . ."

"What?" I asked, and poked my head out so that I could see properly. I could see exactly what she'd seen. Jamie had walked down the street toward a very pretty blond girl and had just handed her the bouquet.

Boys. I hate them all.

• • •

Later that evening, at the sleepover at TJ's, the girls did everything they could to cheer me up. Mad dancing, telling jokes, feeding me a ton of chocolate, making plans for how I could decorate my room down in Cornwall. I had fallen in love with the décor in TJ's bedroom the moment I set eyes on it. It was done out in the strong colors of the East—red, orange, ochre, deep yellow—and the whole effect looked exotic and yet cozy. I could just see my room in the same rich vibrant shades, and Izzie and TJ said they could show me some great shops in Camden Lock where I could get the right extras like cushions, lamps, and sari-type curtains. I tried my best to be animated about it all and not let on that deep inside I was gutted about having seen Jamie with the other girl earlier. I knew that there was nothing any of them could do, and I didn't want my being upset to ruin my first night with them up in London, or for them to think I was some kind of miserable loser that whinged on. Plus the fact that I had made my resolution earlier in the day after talking to Jen—that I was going to live my life to the fullest and not dwell on the bad.

"It was no big deal," I said, putting on my best smile. "I wasn't really *that* into Jamie. It doesn't matter that he's given some other girl flowers. So what? It wasn't as if we were engaged to be married or had been going out with each other for ages or anything."

"Good for you," said Nesta. "I think I would have chased after him and slugged him one."

Izzie and Lucy had wanted to go and confront Jamie then and there, but I had pulled them back. I didn't want to make a scene and I didn't want to fall out with him. On the way home, Izzie kept saying that there might be some explanation, but I didn't think so. I kept remembering that he had said that I was the first girl he had ever bought flowers for, but he seemed pretty pally with the florist. I thought that white roses were going to be *our* flowers. Mine and Jamie's. Something that I would remember all my life. Now I never wanted to see another white rose as long as I lived. They would always remind me of what treacherous, lying, two-timing creeps boys could be.

"He might have been saying sorry for something,"

said Izzie, who for some reason had decided to champion Jamie's defense.

Nesta shook her head. "With a bunch of flowers? No. There's more to it. Honestly it makes me sick the way that boys think they can give us a bunch of flowers and we fall at their feet in gratitude. Well, not me."

Lucy burst out laughing. "You big liar. You're a total sucker for flowers."

"You're the one who's the sucker for flowers," said Nesta. "You should have seen her earlier this year, Cat, when we came back from our school trip to Florence. My brother, Tony, was waiting at the airport for her with a bunch and she just fell at his feet."

"Did not," said Lucy. "Did nooooot. And you *know* I didn't. Honestly, you're such a wind-up."

I had heard all about Nesta's brother and how he and Lucy had something really special—like I had thought that I had with Jamie.

"Just forget him," said TJ. "You're worth more than some stupid boy who sends flowers to girls all over the place and thinks that's all he needs to do.

Somewhere out there is a much nicer boy who will treat you properly."

"I know, I know," I said. "And I know that I said I hate all boys before, but I don't actually. I know there are some nice ones out there. Mac and Squidge, for instance, they're both great."

"I think Izzie would agree with that, wouldn't you, Iz?" teased Nesta.

Izzie stuck her tongue out at her. "Maybe," she said with a smile.

"And the boys you know sound fab too," I continued. "I know there are some boys who are users and players, too, just . . . I didn't think that Jamie was one of them."

"Shame you weren't with us today, Nesta," said Lucy, then turned to me. "Nesta's our resident boy expert. She can spot a player or a user a mile off. She'd have known exactly what type of boy Jamie is just by looking at him."

"True," said Nesta. "In fact . . . hmm . . . that gives me an idea . . .'

9 Lookalike Me

"I'm not so sure that this is a good idea," I said as Nesta, TJ, and I hid behind a phone booth in Holland Park the next day.

"Relax," said Nesta. "You said he likes a laugh, and if the worst comes to the worst and he sees us then we can say we were doing what your mate Becca suggested—surprising him."

I wasn't so sure now that I was outside his house like some stalker. Not only that, but we were in disguise. It had been Nesta's idea after Lucy had said that she would know what sort of boy Jamie was in a second. Nesta got it into her head that we should follow him for a little while like spies. Trouble was that our disguises made us look more like mad people than international cool-but-mysterious secret agents. I'd always thought that going under-cover meant blending in with a crowd, but dressed the way we were, we couldn't have stood out more if we'd tried. Lucy and Izzie had gone off to work in Lucy's dad's health shop for the day so TJ, Nesta, and I went to the fancy-dress hire shop near TJ's house in East Finchley before setting off for Jamie's. When we realized that the spy costumes cost thirty pounds each to hire and the Afro wigs were only £4.99 to buy, the wigs won, no contest. So there we were in our shorts, T-shirts, sunglasses—and wild women wigs. Nesta's was blue, mine was lime green, and TJ's was fluorescent pink.

"This is *totally* brilliant," said Nesta as she caught her reflection in the phone booth window. "No one expects a secret agent to look like this. Everyone expects them to wear white macs and French berets, although we can speak in French accents if you like."

It had seemed hysterical when we were in the fancy-dress shop. A great idea. On the Tube on the way here we hadn't been able to stop laughing at how we looked, but now that we were hovering outside the phone booth the comedy element was beginning to wear off, to be replaced by rising panic—plus it was a boiling hot day with not a cloud in the sky and my head was sweltering under the tight wig.

"What does Jamie's dad do?"

"Something to do with finance I think, but his mum and dad are divorced. His dad lives in Scotland most of the time."

"Och aye hey the noo," said TJ.

"We could be Scottish spies instead of French or Russian," said Nesta. "Let's speak in Scottish accents for the rest of the day. Begorra bejabbers, haggis, tartan, kilts . . ."

"You two are bonkers," I said.

"Och aye, Jimmy," said Nesta. "Dunna get your bagpipes in a twist." Then she began to dance the Highland Fling.

"Er, remind me what we're doing here again," I asked as an old lady went past and gave her a peculiar look.

Nesta stopped dancing and put her arm around me. "Relax, ma petite Scottish amie. Don't worry. We are simply checking out Jamie to see if he is worthy of you or not—but in the meantime, I 'ave to find ze toilet for ze ladies, because I need to gooooooo . . ."

TJ gave her a quizzical look. "That doesn't sound Scottish."

"It's mixed. Scottish and Russian," said Nesta. "I like to keep an open mind."

"Confused, more like," said TJ. "Let's agree. Scottish, okay?" Suddenly she ducked down behind the phone booth and pulled Nesta and me with her. "Someone's coming out of the house. A boy. Is that Jamie?"

I poked my head up so that I could see. It was him. Right on time. Becca had done her homework and phoned his mate Henry last night to find out Jamie's movements for today. Of course Henry wanted to know why we were interested, so Becca had to fill him in and make him promise not to spill the beans. He told us that Jamie was heading out to meet him in Covent Garden at noon.

Our plan – or should I say, Nesta's plan—was that we waited until Jamie came out of the house and then we casually started walking toward him so that Nesta could get a good look at him. He wouldn't know Nesta or TJ but would probably stare anyway, partly because they both have great legs, but also because of the colorful wigs. I was to be in the middle of them and, hopefully, he would do a double turn when he realized that it was someone who looked like me, and then he would realize that it really *was* me, not a lookalike me. This was the crucial point of the plan, because Nesta said that she would be able to tell from his reaction to seeing me exactly what his feelings were for me. I hoped that she was right and that he wouldn't phone the police to report that aliens had landed in West London and were heading straight for him.

Jamie turned out of his gate and began to walk toward us. He was dressed in jeans, his grey hoodie and sunglasses and was looking very cool and grown up.

"Get up, you two," I urged. "He won't know you so I don't know why you're hiding."

"Oh, right," said TJ, and got up and adjusted her wig that had gone a bit squiff.

"Hey, he's a cutie," said Nesta as she got up and pulled me with her.

It was so weird. I'd been looking forward to

seeing Jamie again for ages. Imagining how it would be. Where it would be. But now that it was actually happening, I wanted the ground to open up and swallow me. It was all a big mistake. I looked a total prat. Why on earth had I let the girls talk me into this, never mind wearing this mad wig? There was no guarantee at all that Jamie would find it a laugh—in fact, he might not even be pleased to see me. As I watched him approach us, I realized that actually I didn't know him that well at all. We had only spent a couple of hours together on the trip to Morocco and, although he had seemed like a nice guy and was keen on me there, he looked much more sophisticated than I remembered. I knew he went to private school, but now that I'd glimpsed where he lived as well, I could see that we were from very different worlds. He was going to think this whole idea was so childish. Oh God, oh God, never again, I thought as we began to walk toward him. Already he was staring—and who could blame him? I thought, as I began to blush as pink as TJ's wig.

"Actually, I don't want him to see me like this,"

I whispered, and tried to steer the girls off in another direction while at the same time hiding my face so that he wouldn't see me. Hopefully with the sunglasses and the wig, he wouldn't recognize me at all and we could get back to TJ's and forget the whole thing.

Too late. He was making a beeline for us.

"Hey, girls," he said as he got closer. "It's a bit early for the Notting Hill carnival."

"Vot carnival do you speak of, Eengleesh boy?" drawled Nesta in a heavy Russianish accent.

"I *thought* we were being Scottish," said TJ in a perfect Irish accent.

Jamie looked like he was going to burst out laughing—and then he saw me and screwed his eyes up as if to focus more. As planned, he did a double-take. Then he came closer. "You look like someone I . . . hey . . . Cat, is that you under there?"

"Cat? Me? No. Probably someone who looks like me . . . I mean her . . ." I blustered.

"Surprise," chorused TJ and Nesta.

"Yeah—surprise," I said. "I . . . we . . . that is . . ."

I couldn't deny the fact that Jamie looked

delighted and immediately wrapped me in a big bear hug. "Cat Kennedy! This is fantastic. Wow . . . but you look . . . strange."

I was lost for words, caught between being happy to see him and wondering if I ought to explain.

Luckily Nesta took over. "We've heard a lot about you," she said. "I'm Nesta and this is my mate TJ. And er . . . I couldn't possibly use your loo, could I? I'm dying to go."

Jamie looked totally bemused. "Loo? What? Er . . . Oh . . ." he stuttered as he glanced nervously back at the house. "Er . . ."

Nesta crossed her knees and clasped her hands in the praying position. "Pleeeeease . . ."

Jamie's expression changed from looking delighted to being anxious. He looked studiously at our wigs and then finally nodded. "Come on then, but . . . listen . . . er . . . yeah, great look and all that—but would you mind taking your wigs off before we go in?"

Nesta, TJ, and I exchanged glances as if to say "What's the problem?" but we whipped the wigs off all the same and stashed them in TJ's rucksack. As Jamie ushered us back to the house he glanced at me, but his expression was now impenetrable and I began to wish that I'd never come.

We made our way up the pathway and Jamie opened the front door.

"Only me," called Jamie as we stepped inside a vast white hall with a marble floor.

We heard footsteps approaching from a corridor to our right and then my mouth fell open as a woman dressed in white leotard-and-tights exercise gear appeared. She looked as if she was in her forties, was stick thin and had a shock of red hair. Henna-red hair. In exactly the same style as our Afro wigs, but hers was clearly not supposed to be a joke. Now I understood why Jamie had asked us to take ours off.

"Er, this is a friend of mine, Cat, and her mates . . ." Jamie started.

Nesta stepped forward and shook the woman's hand. "Nesta and TJ."

"Right, Nesta and TJ,' said Jamie. "And this is my mother."

"Do excuse one's attire," she said in a very plummy voice. "I've just had my Pilates lesson." She bent over and touched her toes. "Sooo good for keeping one's back supple."

Ohmigod, I thought as I fixed my gaze on the floor and fought back an irrepressible urge to laugh my head off. I didn't dare look at Nesta or TJ, not even for a second.

10 Mrs. Snob

"AND YOU ARE, AGAIN? I didn't catch it the first time," asked Mrs. Parker as she led us into a magnificent living room off the hall. It must have been about fifty feet long with high ceilings, huge bay windows, and elegant cream furnishings that looked like they cost a fortune. Everything looked as though it had been styled for an interior design magazine photo. Pale duck-blue silk cushions on the two vast sofas were plumped up and arranged so perfectly that I hesitated before sitting down, in case I disturbed the layout. Big art books had been placed on a glass coffee table with carved gold legs. On the floor were immaculate cream carpets that would last five minutes in our house before having something spilled on them.

"Er . . . Catherine Kennedy, but everyone calls me Cat," I said as Nesta came back from the loo and settled next to TJ. As I looked around, I couldn't help thinking that the atmosphere in the house was cold, too formal to be the kind of place where you could kick your shoes off and feel cozy and comfy when you got home. I was going to make my bedroom look exactly the opposite to this grand, immaculate place.

The design was beginning to form in my mind—all the rich warm reds and oranges that TJ had used in her room, with possibly a red velvet throw for the bed. I'd seen one in a mail order catalog at TJ's house and she said that I could borrow it and send it back to her later. For my birthday and Christmas I was going to ask for Moroccan-type knickknacks to finish the look that I wanted, but it shouldn't be hard to create with a couple of pots of paint. All the strong vibrant shades used in hot countries. Plus, there was another reason I wanted to paint those colors. They were the colors from all the countries that Mum had been to, according to her diaries. I think she'd have liked the fact that some of her experiences had inspired me and that, although she was gone, she was still a strong influence on my life. I could hardly wait to get back and get started.

Mrs. Parker looked up to her right, as if scanning an imaginary list. "Kennedy, Kennedy. Hmm? Can't say I know the family. Where are you from, dear?"

"Cornwall," I said as I attempted sit up straight, which was difficult because the sofa was so big and squashy that when I leaned back my feet came up off the floor, making me feel like a five-year-old. I made myself remember what Lucy had said yesterday about that fact that no one can make anyone feel inferior without their permission.

Mrs. Parker regarded me as if I was of a different species to her. "Cornwall? Oh how terribly quaint," she said. "Isn't that where that school friend of yours lives, darling?"

"Ollie Axford," said Jamie.

"Of the Axford family. Jamie is often a guest of theirs, aren't you, darling?" she asked with a brief glance at Jamie before she turned back to me. "But I don't suppose you know them . . . ?"

"Actually, Lia Axford is one of Cat's best friends, isn't she, Cat?" said Jamie.

I nodded.

"Is that so?" said Mrs. Parker, then, as if bored, she turned to Nesta and TJ. "And you girls?"

"Highgate," said Nesta, and was met with an approving nod. "Nesta Williams of the Costello Williams family. Our family goes back years in Spain, Italy, and Jamaica. My father is—" TJ nudged her to shut up.

"I'm from Finchley," said TJ. "Watts family."

"Finchley?" said Mrs Parker, then added disdainfully, "That's North London, isn't it?"

Jamie rolled his eyes. "Mother has never been farther than Hampstead," he explained.

"And you're from Jamie's circle, are you?"

Nesta and TJ shook their heads.

"We go to a public school in North London," said Nesta, and I noticed that TJ looked at her with surprise.

"And I go down in Cornwall," I said. "To the local comprehensive."

"Indeed," said Mrs. Parker, looking taken aback. "Jamie, darling, I don't think you've brought anyone home from a comprehensive before. Still, no matter. I suppose it's good that you mix with all sorts of people."

Jamie looked like he wanted the earth to swallow him up. "Sorry," he mouthed when she looked the other way.

Now I understood why he hadn't been so keen on us coming into his house. Luckily, she lost interest in us pretty swiftly and left to go shower and dress for her ladies' lunch in Knightsbridge.

As soon as she'd gone, Jamie asked us if we'd like anything to drink and disappeared off to get us glasses of lemonade.

"Er, and since when has our school been a public school?" TJ asked Nesta as soon as Jamie had closed the door behind him.

"It's open to the public," said Nesta with a big grin. "And Cat, Jamie's on the level. Not a player or a user, and he clearly adores you. I've been watching him and the way he looks at you. So . . . there has to be an explanation for the flowers yesterday."

She didn't waste any time finding out when he came back. "So, Jamie," she said. "Flowers. Cat tells us that you sent her white roses."

"Yes. You got them okay?"

I nodded. "I left a message on your voicemail. In fact, I left a few messages to let you know I was coming up."

"My phone was nicked a couple of days ago," said Jamie. "I was in a café in Kensington and left it on the table for like, a nanosecond. I looked around and it was gone. Did you try calling the land line here?"

I nodded.

Jamie sighed. "Mum never picks up. She just leaves the machine on the whole time but she's the worst person ever for passing on messages. She listens, then deletes them. Sorry. But I did e-mail you to let you know."

"We've just moved. Not connected up properly yet," I explained.

"I should have known," said Jamie. "But I'm sorry that I didn't know you were coming up. I was going out to get a new mobile just now. I'll give you the new number as soon as I have it. Phew. At least we didn't miss each other. I'd have hated to think that you were up here and we hadn't met up."

"Yes, but never mind all that. Flowers . . ." insisted Nesta. "Do you give many girls flowers?"

"Nesta," warned TJ. "That's not really any of our business."

Jamie smiled and glanced at me. "I don't mind. And no, I don't buy girls flowers as a habit. Only Cat so far, although . . . that said, I did buy my cousin some yesterday to take to a mate of hers in hospital. She's totally broke so don't tell Mum, but I put them on her account. And I got white roses again because, well, I read in a mag somewhere that girls like them, and I think they look classy."

Nesta gave me a smug look and, as Jamie poured the drinks, she gave me the thumbs-up and mouthed, "Sorted." Then she wrapped her arms around herself and started acting out someone being kissed. She looked so silly that I got the giggles, and Jamie turned around to see what I was laughing at and caught her mid-imaginary snog.

"Are you okay?" he asked.

Nesta immediately sat up and coughed. "Oh yes—*uhuh uhuh*—just something stuck in my throat."

The rest of the day was a blast. TJ and Nesta diplomatically made themselves scarce, leaving me to spend the afternoon alone with Jamie. He was so apologetic about his mother and said that she gives everyone the same grilling, which is why he was reluctant at first to introduce us. I said I didn't mind. Which I didn't. We had a great afternoon, what was left of it. We went and bought him a phone, did a bit of shopping in Kensington—where he bought me some gorgeous strawberry-scented soap—and over coffee in Starbucks, I told him of my plans for my room. He asked me to wait for a few minutes while he went to get something. He reappeared later with a carrier bag from Waterstone's bookshop, which he gave to me. Inside was the most fabulous book on North African interiors. It was perfect, full of fantastic ideas for décor.

"We got together in Morocco," said Jamie. "And if you do your room out in those colors, it will be a reminder of our time there. Almost as if you've brought a part of it back with you."

Once again, I felt touched by his thoughtfulness. I'd always thought that Squidge was king of the romantic gestures, but Jamie was a close runner for the crown.

I gave him a big kiss. "Thank you so much. That's the perfect present." It was now doubly confirmed in my mind that I had the right decorating plans.

After coffee, we walked through Holland Park and lay on the grass in the sun for a while. Snogged a bit. Snogged a bit more. He was a really good kisser. Gentle, yet firm at the same time. As we lay in the sun, hand in hand, chatting and kissing, I was so glad that I had made the effort to meet up with him. He was every bit as fab as I remembered. Boys, I thought. I do love them.

By the time I got on the early evening train, even though I had only been away for two days, I felt like I had been away for ages and found myself looking forward to seeing Dad, Luke, Joe, and especially Emma. I was so used to her being there in my life— morning, noon, and night; it was strange to be away from her, even though she could be annoying at times. I hoped that she wasn't pining too much for me. If I ever slept away on a sleepover, she had nightmares and crawled into bed with one of the boys. With me having been away for two days, no doubt she'd have insisted on coming to meet me at the station with Dad, even though it was getting late.

Dad was waiting for me as arranged, but there was no sign of Emma.

"She's happy with Jen at home," Dad told me as he drove us toward the Rame Peninsula, "where we've got a bit of a surprise waiting for you."

"A surprise. What?"

"Ah, it wouldn't be a surprise if I told you, would it? You'll see."

My imagination went into fast gear as I tried to guess what it might be . . . A cat. We'd always talked about getting a cat someday and I knew that Jen was an animal-lover. It was probably most definitely a cat. Or two. Kittens. Fab. I spent the rest of the journey making up names for them. Ben and Boris, if they were boys. Or maybe Buster. Princess and Duchess, if they were girls. No wonder Emma hadn't wanted to come and meet me. She was probably playing with the kittens.

As soon as I walked through the front door, I looked for signs of the cat—but nothing. Ah, I thought, they've probably hidden everything away so that it really is a surprise.

I looked for Emma and found her watching TV in the living room, sitting on Jen's knee.

I held out my arms for her, as usually if I had been away, even if only for a few hours, she would run and cling to me as if I'd been away forever.

"Hey, sausage," I said.

She hardly even looked up. "Shhhh. Watching telly."

Jen smiled at me and rolled her eyes as Emma concentrated on watching some manic cartoon.

Huh, I thought. So much for her having missed me. At that moment, Luke pounced on me and started tying a scarf around my head.

"Wha . . . What are you doing?" I asked.

"Surprise," he said. "Come upstairs."

So that's where the kittens are, I thought, as he led me up the stairs and ushered me along the corridor. I must act like I hadn't guessed, I told myself as I sensed that we were going toward my bedroom.

Suddenly he whipped off the scarf. "Taaadaaah!"

Dad, Luke, and Joe were standing there, grinning like idiots.

"Do you like it?" asked Joe, who was looking very pleased with himself.

"Uh . . . ? But where are they?" I asked as I glanced around the floor.

"Where are who?" asked Luke.

"The cats? The kittens. Ben and Boris."

"Cats? Ben? Boris? What are you talking about?" asked Luke.

And then I looked up and saw the room properly.

"Uh . . ." was all that I could say. They'd painted my room pale blue. Three shades. On the ceiling, the walls, and the woodwork.

"It was Jen's idea after she got back from London," said Dad. "She told us it was your favorite color so we decided to get it ready for your return. The boys haven't stopped for twenty-four hours."

"Uh . . ." I said again. I wanted to storm downstairs and rage at Jen. How *dare* she pick the color for my room? *My* room. Mine. My first ever space and already it had been taken over by someone else and *their* choices.

"Do you like it?" Joe asked with a worried expression.

"Oh . . ."

Luke looked so chuffed with his efforts, and Joe looked so anxious to please, and they had both so clearly done it in the hope of making me happy that I hadn't the heart to tell them that the color they had picked was the last one I wanted. And in a way, they'd got it right. Blue *was* my favorite color. For *clothes*. Not décor. As I looked around, I saw all my great plans for my red Moroccan room evaporate like water. I felt a huge knot of frustration in the pit of my stomach and wanted to cry.

Reversals 11

"SO WHAT ARE YOU going to do?" asked Becca the next day, after she'd had a good look around my room. Lia, Mac, and Squidge had come straight over too, as soon as they heard about the painting fiasco.

"We can repaint it for you," said Mac. "It's completely reversible. Between Squidge and me, if we went at it, it would take a day."

"Although," said Lia, who was sitting on my bed flicking through the Moroccan book that Jamie had bought me. "I have to say, I think it looks great. The pastel color does suit the room. It makes it look crisp and airy, and with the right curtains and cushions, it could look fab. I know you had your heart set on hot spice colors but—I don't think they would have looked right in here. I think they're more suited to an older house and this one is modern. Red and deep oranges would close the space in. Pastels open it up."

"What do *you* want, Cat?" asked Squidge. "It's your room and I know how important this is to you after having shared with Emma all those years. What do you want? Just say the word and we'll transform the place."

"But Luke and Joe would be devastated, never mind the money that Dad forked out for the paint," I said.

"I think he'd understand," said Lia.

"Yeah right," I said. "Like *he'd* be on *my* side. He only cares what Jen thinks these days."

"Okay, tell Jen," said Becca.

"Pfff, her . . ." I snorted. I had hardly spoken to Jen since I was back. This mess was all her fault. All it would have taken was a phone call to ask if I was okay with it—but no, she hadn't even thought to ask. She had bamboozled her way into my room, just like she had the rest of the house, and was slowly taking over. All the bonding that had happened up in London had gone out of the window as far as I was concerned, and she was on my "to be avoided" list—something that was proving difficult to do because unfortunately, as her chief bridesmaid,

I was supposed to be organizing her hen night and had to keep asking her for her girlfriends' phone numbers and what sort of food and drink she wanted. She was in a weird space anyway. Snappy and impatient. Not only that, because of her I was in the doghouse with Dad. Just because I hadn't fallen on the floor and done the "I'm not worthy thank you so much O almighty Jen" act, he'd called me an ungrateful little madam. Me! What a cheek! I never *asked* anyone to paint my room. And certainly not blue!

I reached down under the bed and pulled out the trunk.

"Ohmigod. Your mum's trunk," said Becca. "Can we look?"

I nodded. I had told them what was in there, but this was the first time that any of them had actually seen for themselves, and I noticed Squidge hold back. He knew my mum well and she had always had a soft spot for him. We exchanged a quick look as if to acknowledge that, out of all of them, Squidge understood best what finding the trunk had meant to me.

Soon the four of them were poring through the files, photos, and diaries, and at one point, Lia's eyes filled up with tears.

"I can't bear to think what you must have been through," she said. "I can't imagine what I'd do if anything happened to my mum or dad."

"Me neither," said Becca as she came across Mum's travel file and flicked through. "Wow. Seems your mum went all over the place."

"I know," I said. "I never even knew. I think she must have given it all up when she got married and had kids. Seeing those notes and diaries from her time traveling was part of the reason that I had my heart set on painting my bedroom in the colors from Morocco. A place we had both visited, even if it was at different times. It would be in memory of her. To let her know that even though we have moved from the old house that she is still my mum and always will be. It was a way of bringing part of her here. Her influence at least."

"Wow," said Mac. "That's such a great idea."

"So what are you going to do?" asked Becca again.

"Dunno. But first, tell me honestly, what do you think of the color scheme?"

Becca looked awkward. "Actually I have to agree with Lia. I like it but now, having heard what you just said, I totally understand why you'd want to use the colors from the places that your mum went. They're all the colors of the sun, aren't they? I think you should absolutely definitely paint over the blue now, even if it does look good."

"Mac? What do you think?"

"Oh God, I don't know now. You girls are so complicated. What do you want me to think?"

I laughed. That was such a typical Mac-type response. He was so worried about saying the right thing sometimes. I went to play-throttle him. "Mac, give me an opinion or you die!!!"

"Okay, okay. Do it Moroccan for your mum."

"Squidge?"

"I'm with Lia. I think your brothers, or Jen or whoever it was, chose a good color and you could make it work once you've got a few of your things around. I . . . I might have an idea of how it could look totally fab, so let me get back to you."

I groaned. "Now I really am confused," I said. "Two for, two against. I don't know what I think anymore. What am I going to do?"

"Live with it for a while," said Lia. "And in the meantime, don't get mad or anything or take it out on Jen, as I doubt she meant to annoy you. I think she was trying to do something nice for you. You being cross with her is a total waste of energy because it's not as if it can't be changed."

I do love Lia. She's so sensible and, after they'd all gone, what she had said about Jen got me thinking. We'd had such a good time in London and now that I'd calmed down a bit, I could see that of course she had meant my room being painted as a nice surprise. And what had I done? Blanked her and acted like a spoiled princess. She wasn't to know all my plans as I'd never said anything about them to her. She wasn't to know about Mum or her travels or her trunk. And there was me going on about Dad being the one who doesn't communicate, when all along it was really me who had been holding back.

The house felt quiet after Lia, Squidge, Becca, and

Mac had gone, and I was about to go back up to my room to text Jamie when I heard sniffling coming from the living room. Thinking that it was Joe, Luke, or Emma, I went in to see what was the matter.

Jen was sitting at the table by the open patio doors with her back to me, but I could tell by the way that her shoulders were slumped that she was unhappy about something. She turned when she heard my footsteps and straightened up. I could see immediately by her red eyes that she'd been crying. Oh God, I thought. This is my fault.

"Oh, Cat, I thought you'd gone with your friends," she said with an attempt at a smile.

I shook my head. "I'll join them later. I've still got a few things to do in my room. Where's Dad and everyone?"

"Gone to get some things from the shop," she said.

I went over and sat at the table opposite her and took a deep breath. "Jen, I'm sorry. I've been a cow."

Her face crumpled and she bowed her head. "No. *No.* I'm sorry. I'm so stupid. I should have waited. Checked with you. You're almost fifteen, of course you have your own ideas for your room. I'm such an idiot. I've always been like this. Aries. Always jumping in without looking."

I smiled back at her. "Hey, don't forget I'm Aries, too. Bummer of a sign when it comes to being careful or taking the slow lane."

She half-smiled back. "Yeah. Bummer."

"Is that why you were crying?"

She twisted her hands. "Yes. No. Maybe . . . I don't know, Cat. It's all happening so fast and I . . . and I . . ." She started to sob again and looked so upset that my heart went out to her. I got up and went to sit next to her and put my arm around her. "Hey, hey, Jen. What is it? Don't cry. I can explain why I reacted about the room."

As she continued to sob, I told her all about finding Mum's trunk and her travel diaries, the whole story . . . "So that's why I threw a wobbly," I said. "But you weren't to know. I should have told you about it. And the others. It's me who should be sorry."

My explanation only made Jen cry more. "Sorry, *sorry*," she said. "Don't know what's the matter with me today. Least, I do. Oh God, Cat. Can you ever forgive me? I feel worse than ever about it now that you've told me about your mum."

"You weren't to know. But what about you? Can you forgive me for acting like a spoiled brat?"

"You will never be a spoiled brat, Cat. You haven't got it in you." She took a long sigh. "Oh, what a mess . . ."

"What do you mean?" I asked. "Is there something else bothering you?"

Jen's face crumpled again. "Only . . . everything. I . . . I don't know if I'm ready for all this." She gestured round the room. "I'm getting married in just over a week's time and, apart from the dress and the ceremony, nothing is planned. In all the commotion I . . ."

"What? Hey, Jen, it can't be that bad."

"But it *is*. The worst possible thing that could happen has happened. In all the commotion I forgot to confirm the reception date. I thought it *was* confirmed. I really did. I thought they understood that it was definitely on, but I was supposed to have sent a deposit check a month before the date.

I didn't know or didn't remember them telling me if they did. Apparently they called my old flat, but of course I haven't been there so they canceled my booking and gave the rooms to someone else. Oh, God. I've just been on the phone to them. What am I going to tell your dad? He's going to think I'm so stupid but—I didn't know. I thought that it was all sorted. Oh, God. I should have checked, though. Stupid, stupid me. My head's been somewhere else—moving house and painting rooms blue when it wasn't wanted. It's all too much, this new chapter. It's all too much and I don't think I can cope. I can't get anything right."

I gave her a hug. "Well, what did you expect in a *new* chapter?"

"Everything to be PERFECT!" she said, and attempted to laugh, but it came out more like a hiccup and I could see that she was really stressed. "Oh, I don't know, Cat. It's not just the fact we have nowhere to have the reception now, it's also that I don't know if I'm ready for this new life. Husband. New house. Wedding. I'll be Mrs. Kennedy. Stepmother to four kids—sorry, I didn't mean to insinuate that you were a kid, but oh, you know what I mean. Stepmother. She's always the baddie, like in the *Snow White* story, isn't she? Anyway, I'm not up to the job. I don't think I can do it. I'll be a terrible wife. A terrible stepmother. I don't think I've even grown up yet, and on top of all that I thought you hated me . . ."

"Well, I don't," I said as I gave her a big squeeze. "It's all been new for me, too. But you'll be great, Jen. You are great. We'll be great. We'll work it out."

Jen sniffed. "Do you think?"

I nodded.

"But look. See. This is proof of how rubbish I am. I'm the grown up and yet here I am being comforted by you. Shouldn't it be the other way round?"

"Not necessarily," I said. "Anyway, you're not my mum and you don't have to be. I don't want that."

Jen put her hand over mine. "I know. I've been so aware of that, desperately trying not to overstep the mark. I know I could never take your mum's place, but I do want to be there for you and Luke and Joe and Emma as well as your dad—that is, if you'll let me. I want to be here if you need me."

"And me for you, Jen. I think we can be good friends if we try."

We sat for a few moments with our arms round each other and I felt all the warmth that I'd felt in London for her come flooding back. Of course it was a huge move for her. Dad, Luke, Joe, Emma, and I had lived together forever, and although we had moved house, it wasn't as if we needed to get used to living with five new people like Jen had. It had by far been more of a change of life for her and I hadn't even considered that until now.

After a while, Jen blew her nose and looked over at me. "Cat, do you think . . . do you think I could possibly have a look at what you found in the trunk? I've never really seen pictures of your mother as your dad keeps them so private. I know nothing about her and she's such a major part of all of your lives that I'd like know more about her, who she was, what she was into."

"Of *course*," I said. "I'd love that too. Come on up. And Jen?"

"Yes?"

"Don't tell Dad just yet about the reception plans falling through."

"But why not? I have to tell him sometime. Maybe we could have it here or something? Get a tent?"

"Maybe," I replied, "but I'd like to help. I know the area really well so let me check out a couple of options—that is, if you don't mind. There's *me* being the Aries, jumping in. But I'm sure I could find somewhere for you—and I am the chief bridesmaid after all."

"Okay," she said, "but . . . don't do anything or book anywhere without talking it over with me first, hey?"

We both burst out laughing as we realized how alike we were, and I put my hand out to high-five her. "That can be the first rule we agree for living together. Always talk plans over before doing anything."

Jen high-fived me back. "Suits me," she said. "And by the way, if you want to ask that boy from London to come to the wedding, please do—and any of those new friends of yours. I want you to enjoy the day as much as your dad and I."

"Thanks, Jen," I said, and had to bite my lip from telling her that I'd already asked all of them. I'd taken it for granted that they'd all be welcome. Phew, I thought, us Aries girls really do have to be careful not to leap before we look. Or do anything for that matter.

We went up to my room and, for the second time that day, I pulled out the trunk. I could tell that it meant a lot to Jen that I was showing it to her, and it felt good to be sharing what I'd found out about Mum and not hiding it away like some dark secret not to be spoken of.

Panic

"OH GOD, OH GOD, oh God," I groaned to Lia and Becca as I ran round our kitchen getting out glasses, forks, knives. "We'll never be ready in time and it's my own stupid fault. If I hadn't acted all Mrs. Strop Bottomy with Jen over my room, I'd have had all this organized ages ago."

"Calm down and stop acting like a headless chicken," said Becca.

"Well, it is a hen night," I said, and started clucking and flapping my arms as much like a chicken as I could. Lia and Becca cracked up then and began clucking round the kitchen as well, and we were soon joined by Emma, who on hearing the commotion came in to see what was going on and joined in with great enthusiasm.

It was the Friday before the wedding and ten of Jen's friends were arriving in just over an hour's time. Dad had been packed off down the pub. Luke and Joe were staying over at a friend's and Emma had been allowed to stay because she insisted that she was one of the girls. She begged to be able to wear her bridesmaid's outfit and in the end Jen gave in.

"You're very dressed up tonight," said Lia, when Emma first appeared in it and gave us a twirl.

"It's my wedding dress," she said. "And tonight is part of the wedding."

I can't argue with that, I thought and made a mental note to take it to the dry-cleaner's before the big day. The "things to do before the wedding" list was growing longer and longer, with number one still being: *Find place for reception or else we'll all be out in the back garden.*

"Who's coming?" asked Lia.

"Bunch of Jen's work mates," I said, "so don't feel that you have to stay. They're mostly in their thirties, so will probably just want to sit about drinking and talking about work."

"No prob," said Lia. "Where's the list of to do?"

"By the fridge," I said. Lia and Becca had been

brilliant in coming over to help me organize things for Jen. I hadn't known what to do, but Jen assured me that all they'd want was some food and drink and everything would be okay. It all sounded deadly dull to me, but it was her night so her choice.

"Wine," read Lia.

"In the fridge, but oh—open some red to steam or breathe or whatever it has to do."

"Mixers?" asked Lia. "Girls often like girlie drinks. I know this from doing the bar for Mum at her dos. You need plenty of ginger ale and Coke and lemonade and juice for anyone who's driving."

"They've hired a van and a driver," I said. "I don't think any one of them is driving. Oh God, crisps. Peanuts."

"Sorted," said Lia as she held up bowls full to the brim.

We'd sent Jen upstairs to pamper herself and get ready in leisure so that she could enjoy the night, and I'd thought it was all under control until we started putting things out. I couldn't find anything. The corkscrew. Ashtrays. Did we have enough glasses? There were boxes shoved away in cupboards that still needed to be unpacked.

Lia and Becca told me to sit down, take a few breaths, and polish a few glasses while they took over.

They soon had things organized.

Half an hour later, the house looked lovely— candles on the shelves (even though it was a warm August evening and still light outside, we drew the curtains so it looked atmospheric), the rooms were sprayed with jasmine scent, the white wine was cooling, red wine breathing, nibbles were in their bowls, some gentle background music on the CD player, and we were ready for the guests.

Lia took me to one side. "You know the boys were arranging a little surprise," she said. "Um . . . well, let me just say that Jen might not be the only one who's surprised."

"Meaning?" I asked.

Lia just tapped the side of her nose. "You'll find out," she said with a laugh.

"I think the ladies are here," said Becca as she looked through the window at a van that had just drawn up outside.

I took a deep breath and prepared myself to be on my best behavior for Jen's middle-aged work colleagues.

Two minutes later, ten wild girls burst through the door. They had pink feather boas round their necks, little pink bunny ears on their heads, and a couple of them had wands—which of course had to be handed over to Emma, who suddenly looked perfectly dressed for the occasion.

"Let the party begin," called a tall blond girl with very low cleavage. "Where's Jen?"

Jen appeared at the top of the stairs. "Hey, Carole, Marcie, Trace. Hey . . ."

In a second, she was down the stairs, everyone was air-kissing, and someone whipped out a veil and tiara and put it on Jen's head. Another girl added some pink Velcro handcuffs and another a plastic ball and chain. These girls looked like fun.

Lia was right about the drinks, and large jugs of fruity cocktails were made and were soon circulating as the noise level grew louder and louder. My "tasteful" background CD was taken off and replaced by Bruce Springsteen, then the Rolling

Stones, and the girls were up and boogieing for Britain.

"Er . . . I thought you said they were going to be a boring lot," said Becca with a grin as we watched from the kitchen. "They're like a bunch of hyperactive eight-year-olds who have had too much sugar!"

"I know. Hey, I hope we're this boring when we're as old as them," I said. "Care to join in and dance, madam?"

"Don't mind if I do," said Becca, and we went to join Lia, who was ballet dancing with Emma in the middle of the dance floor. Like the chicken-clucking earlier, everyone caught on, and soon everyone was pirouetting and attempting balletic leaps all over the place.

It was a hoot and after a good hour or so of crazy dancing then singing their heads off, the girls gave Jen presents. They'd bought her some fab stuff, from the naughty to the nice: frames for her wedding pics, pretty silk underwear for the honeymoon, perfumed soaps, scented candles, books on how to keep a marriage alive, a chocolate willy . . .

"Your dad's going to love those," said Becca as Jen unwrapped a pair of edible banana-flavored boxer shorts.

"I do *not* want to know," I said as I put my hands over my eyes.

After presents, one of the girls organized games, and we played charades, musical statues, and we were just getting ready for a game of musical chairs when the doorbell rang.

"Oh God," said Jen. "If any of you have ordered a stripper, I will kill you."

Lia and Becca looked sheepish and went to open the door. A hand passed a portable CD player to Lia, who pressed a button on it. Immediately, the music from the stripping scene in the film *The Full Monty* began to play.

"Oh *noooooo,*" said Jen. "You have."

I put my open palms up to her as if to say, "Nothing to do with me," then I turned to watch with the others.

They weren't your run-of-the-mill strippers. In came Squidge, Mac, Ollie, and—Ohmigod! I could hardly believe my eyes!—Jamie. He looked over at me straight away and grinned sheepishly.

Becca nudged me. "Surprise," she said. "He came down to stay with the Axfords yesterday. When Ollie told him that the boys were doing this, he told us not to tell you that he was going to be here too."

The boys had hats, scarves, coats, fleeces, and wellies on, and must have been absolutely boiling as it had been a hot day. The girls stared clapping to the music and the boys went into a dance routine that had clearly only been rehearsed a couple of times. It didn't matter, because they were hysterical. Squidge and Mac would dance off in one direction while the others went the other way, Ollie seemed to be doing his own thing like he was center stage and Jamie had no rhythm at all. They were vaguely in time with the music though. When Squidge gave the signal, off came the caps, then the scarves . . .

Jen and her mates started calling, "Off, off, off," and stamping their feet. Even Emma joined in.

Off came the fleeces, the jeans . . .

At this point Squidge and Ollie were having a whale of a time, strutting their stuff like professional dancers up and down the room. Squidge twirled his T-shirt in his hand and threw it at one of the girls with a cheeky wink. Ollie wiggled his hips as he pulled his T-shirt over his head. Hmm, nice six-pack, I couldn't help but think. Mac and Jamie, on the other hand, looked like they wanted to die, and I couldn't help but laugh at the embarrassed expressions on their faces as they thrust their hips and tried to look the part.

"Off, off, off . . ." demanded the girls, and at last the four boys were down to nothing more than their swimming shorts, white bow ties around their necks, and their wellies. They lined up at that point, turned round, bent over, and wiggled their bums at us.

Squidge got up and turned round. "And that, ladies, is your lot."

"Teasers," called one girl and, for a moment, her and her friend looked like they might jump on the boys and strip them completely.

Luckily, they were saved as Jen stood up—rather

shakily, as she had been laughing so much. She went to the front door and turned back to us, then thrust her arms up in the air. "Con*ga*!" she called, and began to jiggle her hips and sing the conga tune, "Dad da dad da da da daaa . . ."

Suddenly it seemed the perfect thing to do. In an instant, everyone was on their feet and in a line with their hands on the person in front's hips and off we wiggled and swayed, left leg out then right leg out. Jamie made a beeline for me so that I was in front of him, then off down the road toward the village we went, singing at the top of our voices, past the pub where Dad was sitting in the window. He did a double take as we conga-ed by like lunatics and I gave him a wave. At one point, I swear I saw Mr. Gibbs from the local paper stare at us open-mouthed from the pavement, then I saw a flash. He must have taken a picture as we danced back up the hill and back into the house.

It was a great night. The best hen night ever, all the girls said later as they staggered into the van to be whisked away to their beds. And all the more perfect for me because Jamie had been there and was clearly as into me as he ever had been. After a promise to see him the following afternoon, Mac and Squidge also disappeared off home in the back of Mr. Squires's van, and Mr. Axford came to give Ollie, Lia, Jamie, and Becca a lift.

Jen put her arm around me as we surveyed the mess that was left. "Let's do it in the morning," she said. "And thanks for organizing that."

"No prob," I replied. "Bachelorette party completed. No broken bones. Everyone intact . . ."

Jen rubbed her head. "Just about."

"All we need now is somewhere to hold the wedding reception."

Jen groaned. "Oh don't . . . I'd forgotten about that for a moment. One thing at a time. One thing at a time!"

13 Headline News

I TRIED THE WHITSAND Bay Hotel. It was booked solid.

The Penlee Point Hotel. Also booked solid.

I tried as far down the coast as Seaton and Downderry, but with no luck. I tried all the hotels I knew inland and one receptionist even laughed at me. "You want to book for next Saturday? It *is* the height of the season," she said. "Most people book for these types of events at least a year ahead."

I enlisted Lia and Becca to help, but even with the three of us phoning around we couldn't seem to find anything.

"Booked, booked, booked," said Lia as she showed me the list she'd tried.

"There's a barn in St Austell that could hold a hundred," said Becca, "but you have to arrange your own caterers and it would take too long to get down there really, wouldn't it?"

I nodded. "We need somewhere local, but the catering problem is solved. Mac's mum is going to do it. Remember she used to do big parties when they lived up in London? Mac said it will be a doddle for her and she's delighted to have the work, even at such short notice. All we need is somewhere to hold eighty people."

Next we researched companies that supplied tents, but as with the hotels, it seemed like the whole world wanted to get married in August and all of them were already hired out.

"We could chance it," I said, "and not have a tent—but it would be Murphy's Law, wouldn't it? That would be the day we'd have torrential rain."

"But really, Cat," said Becca, "this isn't your responsibility. You should be hanging out with Jamie now that he's down here, not stuck on the phone. This is your dad and Jen's problem. This new phase of your life was meant to release you from taking care of everyone, but you've ended up doing it more than ever."

"I *want* to do this for them," I said. "They deserve somewhere nice for the reception. And I have seen Jamie. Lots. In between trying to get this organized. And life *will* be different once things settle down, but the move and the wedding are the start of this new phase. I so want everything to go smoothly, and Dad and Jen are looking for places, too. They don't know I've been spending so much time trying to find somewhere. See, I think they've given up, because they've been saying that as a last resort we can have it at home—but it won't be that special, will it?"

"Let me go and talk to my mum," said Lia, and secretly I breathed a sigh of relief. I had been hoping that she might say this, because if anyone could sort this out, it would be Mrs. Axford. She was an ace at organizing parties, but I hadn't wanted to impose in case she might think that I was taking advantage of her good nature. She always invited me and the rest of the gang up to any social events up at Barton Hall, and provided us with costumes on the night if it was fancy dress, then afterwards she'd load us down with leftover party food. I didn't want her thinking that I took any of it for granted.

Just after Lia left to go and find her mum, Squidge called.

"Come over right now," he insisted.

"Why, has something happened?"

"Nope. Just get yourself round here."

"Oh, tell me now, Squidge," I said but he'd hung up.

"I'd like to kill him when he does that," I said to Becca, "demanding that I turn up then not telling me why, and then my mind goes into overdrive trying to imagine what he wants."

"Mine, too," said Becca. "So let's get over there."

We got on our bikes and whizzed down to the village as fast as we could, and once there, his mum directed me up the stairs where Squidge was sitting at his computer. He glanced at his watch. "Hmm. Not fast enough," he said. "When I summon my minions, I expect them to get here in record time."

I glanced over at Becca and she nodded. Together we pulled Squidge off his chair and onto the carpet.

"No, no," he cried. "My leg, my arm, don't forget my broken bones . . ."

Becca pinned him down. "Your pathetic excuses no wash with us, *signor*," she said in a Spanish accent. "You 'ad the plaster off ages ago."

Squidge held his hands over his face. "Okay. Do what you must, but I vill never tell you my secrets. You may torture me, do your vorst but please I beg you, don't ruin my beautiful looks."

"Becca, let him up," I said. "Come on, enough messing about. What do you want?"

Becca did as I asked and Squidge sat back at his computer, pressed a few buttons, then scrolled down to find an Internet site. "I didn't want to describe this to you on the phone, Cat, in case it didn't sound as fab as it looks—but take a deco at this . . ."

He stopped scrolling on a page showing the interior of a room, then turned to gauge my reaction.

"Ohmigod," I said as I stared at the picture on the screen. "Squidge, you're an angel."

"Aren't I?" He beamed back. "And it's Moroccan, too."

It was perfect. A room in Marrakech. The walls

were painted the same sky-blue as mine in my bedroom at home, but the designer had used burnt orange to contrast with the blue and it looked absolutely fabulous. The windows and door were painted orange, rusty-orange silk curtains floated at the window, and various knickknacks had been chosen to complement the color scheme.

"I thought I'd seen something like this," said Squidge, "when Lia first started talking about the Moroccan trip, and I researched the locations on the Net. I didn't want to say until I was sure I could find it again."

"Amazing you remembered it," I said.

"It struck me at the time as a great use of color. You don't always have to have orange or red walls to make a room look exotic. In fact a lot of designers use white walls in hot countries, but with the right rugs, cushions, and lamps, you can make it look totally Moroccan."

Squidge knew about stuff like this, and was into color and design, because he wants to be a film director or a photographer when he leaves school. I gave him a big hug.

"Can you print it for me?" I asked.

Squidge nodded, pressed a few buttons, and the picture began to print out. "If you go to one of the big DIY stores, they have all sorts of paint effects you can buy now, and I bet you could get one that makes the paint look cracked like old wood, which would look fab in burnt orange. Mac and I will help you do it if you like."

"I'd love it," I said. "Maybe after the wedding?"

"Just say when," said Squidge, "and we shall make your room just how you wanted."

Squidge is such a good mate and I knew that he wouldn't rest until he knew I was happy with the result. At least that's one thing sorted, I thought as he printed out the color scheme for me. My room was going to look brilliant after all.

"I wished that there was something I could do for you in return," I said. "What can I do?"

Squidge shrugged. "You don't have to do anything. I . . ."

"I know," I said as an idea struck me. "How are you getting on with your bike?"

Squidge groaned. "I'll get round to it one of these days."

"Today then!" I said. "You can do it, Squidge."

"I know, just . . . Mac and Lia have been trying to get me to do it and watching my every move, but they don't realize they make it worse."

"I won't look," I said. "You can fall off as many times as you like. And anyway, we learned to ride bikes together, don't you remember?"

"Yeah, come on. We're your oldest friends," said Becca. "Least, Cat is!"

Squidge sighed and got up. "I suppose—and if I can't make a fool of myself in front of my oldest friend, then who can I?"

We went downstairs and wheeled his bike around from the back shed, and after a few times of him getting on it with us holding the bars, he suddenly said, "Oh, this is *ridiculous*. Let go." And he was off down the road, cycling as happily as he ever did. He stopped the bike, turned around, and pedaled back, no hands, just like he always used to when we were kids. He was about to get up and stand on his seat when his mum came round the corner, waving a paper at us.

She was laughing. "You've got to see this," she said, and ushered us into her kitchen where she spread the paper out on the table.

"Oh. My. God!" I said when I saw the front page.

Local Ladettes On Fun Girls' Night Out, read the headline underneath a big picture in color of all the girls at Jen's hen night in various states of dishevelment and Squidge, Mac, Jamie, and Ollie in their undies. It was hilarious and everyone looked like they were having a whale of a time.

Underneath the photo, Mr. Gibbs had written a scathing article about how modern girls were out binge-drinking at younger and younger ages, which was unfair because Lia, Becca, and I had only had Cokes.

"But it wasn't like that," I said. "We weren't being louts and it was her *hen night*."

"Yeah," said Squidge. "It wasn't as if anyone was sick on the pavement or anything."

Mrs. Squires waved her hand dismissively. "Oh, don't worry about old John Gibbs. He thinks it's clever to have a go at everyone. Typical journalist. Making a story out of nothing."

I hope it does come to nothing, I thought. My teachers and everyone in the village is going to see that paper. I hope they don't all think we've turned into ladettes over the summer holidays.

Mrs. Squires must have seen that I looked worried. "Hey, let it go, Cat, love. Everyone knows you're not a lout."

I tried to tell myself she was right, but it didn't help when Becca and I rode back through the village and a bunch of Luke, and Joe's mates were outside the newsagent's and starting acting drunk and falling over when they saw us.

"Just ignore them," said Becca.

And then Mrs. McNelly from the post office saw us and acted out glugging from a bottle then staggering about.

"Very funny," I said with an attempt to smile.

It didn't stop with her. It appeared that everyone had seen the paper. The lady from the off-license waved at us from the window when we drove past and pointed at a pile of cans of lager. The ladies in the baker's laughed when they saw us and danced a quick conga round the shop.

As we got closer to my house, a silver-blue Mercedes sports drove by and slowed down in front of us. "Oh, probably someone stopping to ask for our autograph," said Becca, "seeing as we're the most famous non-drinking lager louts in the country."

A stunning-looking middle-aged blond lady got out of the car and came toward us. It was Mrs. Axford.

"Hey, you two," she said.

"Hi, Mrs. Axford," we chorused.

"Hey, Cat, Lia told me about your predicament re Jen's wedding," she said, "and I'd love to do what I can to help. I have a company I use up in London and they're used to last-minute requests. I've already spoken to them and they can let us have a tent. One of those red-and-gold Arabian-type ones. Holds about a hundred. Would that do?"

"Oh gosh, yes, that would be perfect. Do you know how big it is exactly, because our garden isn't that huge."

Mrs. Axford smiled her megawatt smile. "How

about we put it up on the beach at the bottom of our garden? You know, where Lia held that Moroccan barbecue for Squidge? Do you think your dad and Jen would like that? It would be so romantic when the sun goes down and there's plenty of parking up at the house for all the guests."

I felt as if I'd won the lottery or something. Suddenly everything seemed to be working out.

"*Like* it? They'd *love* it!" I said. "Thank you so much."

"Pleasure. So that's sorted then," said Mrs. Axford and went back to her car. "Ask Jen to give me a call and we'll finalize details."

"What a day," I said to Becca as the Mercedes started up and drove off. "My room—sorted. Wedding location—sorted. Squidge's fear of getting back on his bike—sorted. It's amazing, isn't it, how things can change? One day everything seems hopeless, then it can all turn around again out of the blue and work out to be better than you ever imagined."

"*Nil desperandum,*" said Becca. "I think that means: never give up or despair, or something like that, as you never know what's around the next corner."

At that moment, a white van came whizzing round the bend. We could see that the man in the passenger seat was reading the local paper. He glanced at his paper, then at us, then back at the paper, then waved out the window. "All right, dahlings?" he called.

I grinned back at him. "Actually I am," I called back. "All right and double it!"

The Big Day

IT WAS THE MORNING of the wedding and the house felt strangely quiet, seeing as it was The Big Day.

Squidge's mum was upstairs doing Jen's hair.

Emma was in her room next door with Jen's best mate, Carole, who was painting her toenails.

Dad had gone off early to get changed at his best man's house.

Joe and Luke had already gone off up to the church at Rame Head, where they were acting as ushers. They'd looked so cute before they went, in their navy suits with their hair brushed, their faces all shiny.

I had been ready for over half an hour.

In my dress.

Makeup on.

Hair blow-dried.

Sitting on my bed.

Quiet. Quiet. Quiet.

I got up and looked out of the window in case the car arrived early, and my pre-wedding butterflies were suddenly taken over by an overwhelming feeling of distress. I found myself taking a looooooong deep breath as if something was happening that was hard to take in. This really was it. Jen would be Mrs. Kennedy, Dad's wife from today on. Not my mum anymore. My Mrs. Kennedy was deceased. Gone. And I felt desperately sad about it. It's strange. So many times I thought that I'd come to terms with her death. Accepted that I'll never see or hear her again—and then it happens, like a tiger jumping unexpectedly out of the bushes at me, I feel knocked over with grief and paralyzed with the finality of it all. The fact that I'll never hear her voice again. See her face. Her smile. She's not coming back. How can people just be there one day and not the next? Where do they go?

I needed to see her. To feel something of hers. So I pulled the trunk out.

As I was looking at the pictures, there was a knock on the door. I'm not going to cover these up,

I thought, I'm not going to pretend that I wasn't looking at them, whoever it is knocking. She was my mum and part of this family, although you'd hardly know it. A couple of days ago, I had finally shown the contents of the trunk to Luke, Joe, and Emma. I thought it was going to be such a big thing for them, but Emma looked at them like she would one of her comics. Interested for a moment, then it was like, so what? Old photos. They could have been of anyone. A stranger. I don't think she grasped their importance at all. Maybe she will later, I told myself. When she's older. Joe didn't seem that bothered either. He flicked through, then shrugged and went back to playing a game on his computer. He was three when she died. Did he remember her at all? Only Luke stayed and went through them. He looked sad. He was five when she died. Younger than Emma is now, but old enough to have some memories. "I wish I could remember more," was all he said before he too left me alone with her relics.

I looked up from the photos as my door opened. It was Jen.

"Hey," she said and tiptoed in. She was still in her dressing-gown, but her hair and makeup were done.

"You look fab," I said. "Don't think much of the wedding dress, though."

She laughed and gave me a twirl. "That would be a laugh, wouldn't it? Turning up like this? Yeah, let's go in our jim-jams. God, I'm neeeeervooooous." She glanced down at the photos and saw what I'd been doing and came and sat next to me on the bed. "Looking at your photos of your mum, hey?"

I nodded. "I was thinking that you'll be Mrs. Kennedy after today."

She put her hand over mine. "I'll be *Jennifer* Kennedy. Your mum will always be *Laura* Kennedy. Actually, Cat . . . I was thinking about all the things you found," she said. "And I have a suggestion. Rather than leaving it all in that trunk under the bed, I was thinking, why don't you do something with it all . . . ?"

"Do something? Like what?" I held my breath. For a moment, I imagined that she might be about to ask me to throw it all out or give me a lecture about letting go of the past.

"Make a journal or an album of some sort," said Jen. "A book of your mum's life—as a tribute to her. Put in examples of her work, her photos, maybe even testimonies from people who knew her. Get in touch with all her relatives and old friends. Ask them for anecdotes. Write them down. Ask them for any photos you maybe haven't seen. And then maybe frame your favorite ones for the house. We can put them wherever you like."

I let out the breath I had been holding in and, at first, I didn't say anything in response. I thought it was the most *brilliant* idea and already my mind had gone into overdrive picking a photo for the cover. Thinking about how I could lay it out. I could get TJ to help, as I know she runs the school magazine at her school up in London and knows about layout and stuff. Squidge could help me photograph her favorite places down here. Yes. What a fab, *fab* idea. I would make it the most beautiful book ever. I knew that later in their lives, Emma, Joe, and Luke *would* want to know more about Mum. It would be fantastic to have it all there, not shoved away, forgotten, unimportant, gathering dust. She was part of all our lives and deserved to be recognized for that.

Jen looked worried. "Oh, God, have I done it again?" she asked. "Overstepped the mark?"

I turned and hugged her. "No. *Nooooo*. Jen, it's the *best* idea I have ever, *ever* heard. Thank you so much. I love it."

Jen looked delighted at my reaction and, for a moment, I saw her eyes shine with tears. It was going to be that kind of a day, I thought, and at that moment, I knew that it really was going to be a good new chapter in all our lives.

"You ready?" I asked as I brushed my own tears aside.

Jen took a deep breath and nodded. "Yes. No. Almost."

"How you feeling?"

Jen let out another long sigh. "Arghhhhhhh. Scared. Nervous. Petrified. Happy. Ready. Almost. Oh *God* . . ."

I stood up and put my hands on my hips. "What we need in this house is music!" I declared. "This place is *way* too quiet for a pre-wedding."

I raced downstairs and found a CD amongst Dad's classic collection from the sixties. I put on the track I wanted and turned the volume up. The sound of the Dixie Cups' "Chapel of Love" rang out of the speakers at full blast: *"Going to the chapel and we're gonna get married. Going to the chapel and we're gonna get married. Gee, I really love him and we're gonna get married. Going to the chapel of love."*

Suddenly there was a commotion in the hall and I went out to see what it was. Emma, Carole, and Squidge's mum had appeared in the corridor, each with a hairbrush in her hand like a microphone. With Mrs. Squires leading the other two, they went into a dance routine, shimmying a couple of steps to the left and then to the right like they had been rehearsing for weeks. They made the most hysterical girl band: tiny Emma in her fairy outfit (back from the dry-cleaner's and pristine again), Carole with her blond hair still in big rollers, and Mrs. Squires in her hairdressing apron. But to the left and right they grooved in perfect time, waving their arms in the air to the rhythm of the song. Jen and I clapped our appreciation, then we all danced up and down the stairs, then along the downstairs hallway, singing at the top of our voices: "*Going to the CHAPEL OF LOOOOOOOVE.*"

Outside, the wedding car tooted its arrival.

"Oh God, I'm not even dressed!" cried Jen, and it was like someone pressed the fast forward button on a DVD, and we all went into top gear getting ready. Jen putting her dress on, Carole taking her rollers out, me applying a last slick of lip gloss and squirt of my Lacoste Touch of Pink perfume.

It was going to be a great day.

"She's here, she's here," called Luke, and ran into the church when the limo drew up outside the church on the lane up to Rame Head.

Jen stepped out of the car and a couple of late-comers stopped to stare and say, "Ahhh."

She looked an absolute picture. Radiant, elegant and immaculate. She smiled at me nervously as she made her way through the little gate and up the path toward the church. Once outside the porch, we stopped, we all took deep breaths, then a grinning Luke and Joe opened the tall doors.

It was time.

As we stepped inside, immediately the music to the song "The Rose" by Bette Midler started up. Dad was standing at the front and turned, and when I saw his expression when he looked at Jen, for the third time that day, I had to choke back tears. The pews were full of familiar faces and, as we walked up the aisle, everyone's smile was on full beam. It was amazing. Like walking through waves of love that were rolling toward us. I had never experienced anything like it and felt my face split into an enormous grin. Most of the village was there, all done out in their best clothes. Even Mr. Miserable Gibbs from the local paper was there, looking on with wet eyes. Dad was a popular member of the community, as Mum had been, and it seemed that everyone was glad to see him happy again after his loss. On the bride's side were Jen's family and all her mates from the hen night, plus a few others. Most of them looked like they were torn between smiling and crying.

On Dad's side were the villagers, a few cousins and aunts and uncles, my new London friends, looking like they'd stepped out of a magazine: Nesta, TJ, Lucy, and next to them the Axfords and Jamie, who wasn't looking at Jen, he was looking at me. At the front, Squidge was videoing the arrival of the bride, Mac beside him taking photos of the guests on the digi-camera. And on the right, Izzie was at a microphone singing "The Rose" with Becca.

It felt like a perfect moment. I glanced over and caught Dad's eye for a second. He looked so young and hopeful and I thought, I really do hope he is happy with Jen. He deserves a second chance. He smiled and nodded before turning toward the altar and the priest, who began to speak.

"Dearly beloved, we are gathered here today . . ."

Dearly beloved. I looked up at the altar and wondered if Mum was somewhere looking down on us. There is so much we don't know, I thought, so much we don't understand, but whatever happens, a part of her will always live on in me and in my memories of her, and I will always cherish them. Yes, she has gone, but she will always be there as an important part of my past. The beginning chapters of my life. In the meantime, I'm still here. We're still here. Dad, Luke, Emma, Joe, and now Jen. My family. I glanced back at the pews where my lovely friends, old and new, were now seated together: Becca, Lia, Mac and Squidge, Jamie, Lucy, TJ, Izzie, and Nesta. They all saw me look round, beamed back at me, and Izzie gave me the thumbs-up.

So much has happened in this holiday, I thought. So much has changed. New house. New stepmum. New friends. It's the end of August. Another week and it will be back to school. Into Year Ten and hopefully lots of good times ahead. I know sometimes my life will still feel like a roller-coaster ride, but that's okay, because that seems to be the way of things as far as I can make out. Up, down, round and round we go through all the changes.

As the priest continued, and Jen and Dad stood facing each other saying their vows, I felt a wave of happiness begin to rise in me. Yes, there would be good times ahead. I could feel it. The past has gone, the future is a closed book, but this present moment is real—and here we are in it, the dearly beloved, all mates together.

Get smitten with these sweet & sassy British treats:

Gucci Girls
by Jasmine Oliver

Three friends tackle the high-stakes world of fashion school.

10 Ways to Cope with Boys
by Caroline Plaisted

What every girl *really* needs to know.

Ella Mental
by Amber Deckers

If only every girl had a "Good Sense" guide!

From Simon Pulse · Published by Simon & Schuster